ALSO BY BRENDAN HALPIN

How Ya Like Me Now

FOREVER CHANGES

307   239

557   383   241   181   179

467   131

311

.

29

313   31

563   389   137   59   13

139   61

317   191   97

251   37

193

569   101   103

479

571   397   197   199

257

33

229 227

173

223

83   167

79

283

47

23   163

7 **FOREVER CHANGES**

19   43   113

41   73   277

71

107   109   157

151   211

269   271

337

BRENDAN HALPIN

Farrar Straus Giroux   New York

Copyright © 2008 by Brendan Halpin
All rights reserved
Distributed in Canada by Douglas & McIntyre Ltd.
Printed in the United States of America
Designed by Irene Metaxatos
First edition, 2008
1   3   5   7   9   10   8   6   4   2

www.fsgkidsbooks.com

Library of Congress Cataloging-in-Publication Data
Halpin, Brendan, date.
    Forever changes / Brendan Halpin.— 1st ed.
        p.   cm.
    Summary: Although encouraged to apply to colleges, Brianna Pelletier, a mathematically-gifted high school senior with cystic fibrosis, dwells on her mortality and the unfairness of life.
    ISBN-13: 978-0-374-32436-0
    ISBN-10: 0-374-32436-0
    [1. Cystic fibrosis—Fiction.   2. Death—Fiction.   3. Mathematics—Fiction.   4. High schools—Fiction.   5. Schools—Fiction.   6. Massachusetts—Fiction.]   I. Title.

PZ7.H16674Fo 2008
[Fic]—dc22

2007026494

For Nan Olson, Jen King, and Deb Bancroft

FOREVER CHANGES

SO...

As the warm sunlight faded, there was a faint chill in the breeze coming off the harbor. Brianna popped a pill, washed it down with water, and ate a tortilla chip. Dad took a long pull on his Corona. They were the only people sitting on the terrace of Captain Cancun's Mexican Ristorante on the Tuesday after Labor Day.

"So," Dad said, and with that one word, she could tell he was about to hit on some topic she didn't want to talk about. That "so," delivered with that expectant tone, was always the way he launched them into some kind of awkward discussion she didn't want to have. "So," he'd say. "Any cute boys in class this year?" or "So. How's the hangover?" or, tonight, "So. When are we going to go college visiting?"

Brianna dipped another chip and looked out at the harbor. Just at the line of the horizon, she could see a boat. As she watched, it disappeared over the horizon, off to sea, off maybe to Spain, where it would end up if it kept going straight from here all the way across the Atlantic Ocean. Except it wouldn't be straight, because the idea of straight on a curved surface was kind of sketchy.

It would actually be a direct line following the curvature of the earth.

"I dunno. I mean, I don't think . . . Melissa wants us to take the commuter rail in so she can have a tour and an interview at BU. So maybe I'll just do that."

"I looked on the Web site. MIT has info sessions twice a day. I really think you should schedule an interview and go, Bri."

Suddenly, the tortilla chips were very interesting. She picked one up, thought briefly that calculating the area of this chip would be difficult because, again, it wasn't a collection of points in a two-dimensional plane, it was a three-dimensional surface with a pronounced curvature. All the better to scoop up the last of the salsa. As she scraped it from the bottom of the white bowl, Brianna decided she didn't want to fight tonight. She was finally feeling better, and even with that little chill in the air reminding her that school was starting in two days, it still felt like summer. She wanted to hold on to this night, this last glimpse of summer, and not screw it up with tears and name-calling and telling Dad what he didn't want to hear. She looked out at the harbor, felt the breeze on her face, and thought she'd probably never see the end of summer again, so it was just easier to say, "Okay, Dad."

Dad's shoulders relaxed. He'd been gearing up for a fight, and she could see the relief on his face. "Thanks," he said.

Brianna smiled. "Least I can do."

Dad said, "Well, we've gotta be up early tomorrow. I guess we should hit the road." Brianna knew he also didn't want her on the back of his bike after dark, but she decided not to bust his chops.

Dad raised his arm to signal the waitress, and the sleeve of his T-shirt slid up slightly, revealing the tattoo of Brianna's name and birth date inside a heart. The waitress came over, and Brianna saw her eyes flit down to Dad's massive bicep. "Anything else for you tonight? Another Corona?" she asked hopefully.

"Not tonight," Dad said. "Driving."

The waitress smiled. "Okay then," she said, gathering up their plates. "Let me just get this out of your way, and I'll be right back with your check."

"Thanks," Dad said.

Brianna looked over to the beach. It was getting dark, and she could see the last few dedicated beachgoers collecting their coolers, blankets, towels, and umbrellas, and heading away from the sea. She fought back a pang of sadness. Every other September she could remember, she'd looked forward to the start of school, the new classes, the new clothes—it had always felt exciting, like everything was starting fresh.

But now she didn't feel like anything new or exciting was starting; she just felt like something was ending.

just not today

The sound of weights clanking together woke her up. It was still dark. She shuffled to the kitchen and got her handful of pills from the Wednesday section of her pillbox. She grabbed a bag of pretzels and a Gatorade.

She plopped on the couch in the living room and turned on the TV. She watched CNN without really taking it in, washing down the pills and pretzels with Gatorade.

Finally the clanking stopped and footsteps approached. "I'm just gonna get showered, hon, okay?"

"Please do. You reek."

Dad smiled. "Nice breakfast there."

"Don't worry—I'll chug an Ensure later."

"Seriously, how can you drink that stuff? What in nature is that color blue? Nothing! It looks like wiper fluid."

"It is. I thought I'd go for a quick exit instead of this long slow decline thing."

"Jesus, Bri, shut up."

"Will you wash up so we can get this over with? I gotta go hang with my best friends today."

"Are you going back to group?"

"Dammit, Dad! Stop asking about the group. I am not going back there." It sucked enough that she had to go to the hospital today. There was no way she was going to a cystic fibrosis support group.

Dad looked sad and turned away without saying anything. Brianna instantly felt bad; she hadn't wanted to fight last night because it was the end of summer, but today was the beginning of real life again, and she was grumpy. "I'm sorry!" she yelled down the hall as he went into the bathroom.

She heard "Forgiven!" in a muffled tone from behind the door, and then the noise of the shower. More yakkity-yak on CNN that she couldn't bring herself to pay attention to.

Dad came into the living room dressed in khakis and a white button-down shirt. She was glad he wasn't wearing the purple vest. He used to put it on when he got dressed, but Brianna told him it was way too dorky and he had to wait until he got to Bargain Zone to wear it. She didn't tell him it was just depressing to see him in that hideous vest.

"Can we turn off the TV?" Dad asked.

"Jeez, Dad, you always seem very interested in CNN when Soledad O'Brien is on."

Dad smiled. "Yeah, well, she's a very talented anchor."

"And she's not on till seven. Fine, how about"—Brianna pushed buttons on the remote—"Dora the Explorer?"

"Fine. As long as it's not friggin' rap videos."

Brianna thought about responding, but she decided she'd grumped at Dad enough for one morning. Dad began the process of percussing her body to loosen the gunk inside. They had vests that could do this stuff for you, but Dad's crappy insurance wouldn't pay for one for a dependent child, which meant she could only get it if she was independent, in which case Dad's crappy insurance wouldn't cover her anyway. So Dad beat her every morning, then turned her over and beat her some more. She got a fair amount of mileage out of this joke—when people asked how her day was, she would often say something like "It started with some huge tattooed guy beating me, so it can pretty much only get better."

Brianna coughed and spat a lump of gunk into a paper towel. "Juicy!" she said.

"Ah, you can do better than that. You call that mucus?" Dad said. "I've seen thicker gunk in ketchup bottles."

Brianna started to laugh, which of course led to coughing, which in turn led to an even bigger gob of mucus being dislodged and spat out.

"Now *that's* what I'm talkin' about," Dad said, smiling. "You driving to your appointments today?"

Brianna rolled her eyes and said, "Of course!"

"Are you sure you're feeling up to it? I mean, we can call for a ride, you know. Cindy's always home, and she said she'd give you a ride anytime you needed it, or I can drive you to the commuter rail. You seem tired. You've been on the couch since you got up."

"Dad, if you made pretty much any teenager get up at five-thirty, you'd see the same thing."

He looked wounded again. "Bri, you know I have to be at the store at seven or I'll—"

"I know, Dad," she said quietly. "I didn't mean . . . I'm sorry, I wasn't trying to make you feel bad. Anyway, I'm driving."

Dad looked like he was about to say something, but then seemed to change his mind. "Listen, it's supposed to rain today, and you know the bridge gets really slippery in the rain, and people always drive like idiots . . ."

"Dad, I'll be fine," Brianna said, exasperated. "Are you riding your bike in the rain today?"

"Yeah, but I'm not driving all the way into Boston." He paused, looking like Brianna had felt last night—like it was just easier not to fight. "Okay, okay. Ask Dr. Patel to call me, will you?"

"Yeah." Dad enfolded her in a hug, and Brianna wondered again how she could share DNA with this guy who seemed about four times her size.

"I love you, sweetie."

"You too, Daddy."

Dad walked out into the garage, pulled on his helmet and jacket, and started his bike.

Brianna watched him roar off down the street, then headed to her car—a Pontiac Sunfire that was ten years old and had 103,000 miles on it. Sometimes Brianna joked that her main hope in life was that her car would die before she did. Nobody laughed at that in group, nobody even gave a little smile like they had thought that too, like they got that they were wearing clothes that somebody would buy at Goodwill when their grieving parents donated them. They were all about Not Letting Cystic Fibrosis Hold

Me Back, and rock climbing and worrying about how to get their scrawny bodies to look good in a prom dress.

She started the Sunfire and drove too fast to the highway. The car had no pickup and was topping out at about sixty-six mph these days, but it could take a corner fast, so accelerating into the turns from her house to the highway was pretty much the only fun it offered her.

There was nothing that could successfully distract Brianna from the feelings that driving down Route 1 into Boston brought up.

She clenched her teeth really hard and tried not to think about sitting in the passenger seat with Dad behind the wheel in a suit, on their way to Molly's funeral at Holy Name Church in West Roxbury six months before. She passed the gigantic cactus outside the steak house and remembered seeing it all blurred through tears, coughing and crying and Dad not saying anything, because what could he say?

When she reached the orange dinosaur at the mini-golf place, the view in her mind suddenly switched. She remembered another trip down Route 1 two months ago, herself in the passenger seat in tears again, this time saying, "I'm next, Daddy, I'm next, I'm not ready," and this time Dad saying, "You're not next, Bri, you're not. You've beaten infections before, sweetie. This is routine for you."

When she got to the Tobin Bridge, she glanced at the water far below. She noted the sign for the jumpers: "Feeling Desperate? Call the Samaritans."

If I ever decide to take a dive off this bridge, she thought, I'm taking this car with me, and there'll be no time to call the Samaritans. She'd done it in her mind a million times—she always saw herself shooting off the edge, flying through the air in slow motion, frozen at the top of the arc for a long second, perfect, like in a movie.

She wondered if she'd make a big splash or if the car would shatter when it hit the water. If she had a pencil, she might be able to calculate the amount of force she would hit with, figuring the Sunfire weighed about a ton, but she didn't know how much impact the Sunfire's frame could withstand, so doing the math couldn't answer her question unless she could fill in that variable. She doubted that was the kind of information Pontiac had on their Web site: here's how much force you can apply to our vehicles before they smash into a million pieces.

She thought not just of the car, but of herself shattering into a million pieces, none of which would ever have to go back to the hospital, none of which would ever have to work so damn hard to breathe.

She reached the tollbooth, paid her three bucks, and kept driving. Maybe someday, she thought. Just not today.

easy for you to say

With traffic and parking and showing her little card and walking past all the concerned parents with their babies in the hospital lobby (and Brianna knew some of them had kissed a salty baby and were praying, please God don't let it be my kid), Brianna had forgotten all about calculating the impact of a Pontiac Sunfire on the surface of the Mystic River by the time she reached her doctor's office and sat down to wait.

She was working on a Sudoku puzzle when suddenly Leila, her social worker, was looming over the edge of the newspaper.

Leila had on so much foundation that she smelled of it. She was wearing a necklace with a huge gold circle that sat right at her collarbone. Her hair was cut short, and she'd had her tips frosted. On her left wrist, she wore a blue rubber BREATHE bracelet, like Brianna and her friends Melissa and Stephanie and about half the people in the waiting room here wore.

"Brianna!" she said. "We've really missed you at group! Is everything okay?"

"Yeah. I've just been busy."

"Well, that's fantastic! Because I know a lot of times after a big hospitalization like that, a lot of people get discouraged, but I really admire the way you dove back into life. You're really courageous, you know."

Brianna forced a polite smile onto her face. "Well, thanks."

"It's my pleasure. So listen, as you probably remember, we have a group meeting today, and I don't know if you—"

"Can't make it. Cheerleading practice. Our new coach thinks we should have double sessions just like the football team, and since I'm already missing the morning session, I can't miss the afternoon's."

Leila's eyes filled with tears and she said, "Cheerleading practice." If Leila wasn't so annoying, Brianna might have felt bad about making her cry with a lie. Leila took a deep breath and added, "Keep fighting, Brianna."

"Oh, yeah, I'm always fighting," Brianna replied in a flat voice.

If Leila noticed, she didn't show it. "You certainly are, kid. Well, listen, I have another appointment, but it's really great to see you. I know you're busy, but I am here to help you. Feel free to call me anytime if you need something, or even if you just want to talk." Behind Leila's professional warmth, Brianna could sense how Leila fed on kids' pain and fear like a vampire, how much she needed for sick kids to tell her how scared they were. It was creepy.

"Well, I do have a question, actually," Brianna said.

"Shoot," Leila said.

"What do you think happens when we die? I mean, where do you think we go?"

She wasn't really sure what made her ask that, but she thought maybe if Leila told her anything that made sense, she'd forgive her for being a creepy vampire, for telling her to keep fighting, and maybe she'd even give group another shot after all.

Leila looked stunned. "Uh, well, I, uh, of course, every tradition has its own . . . I mean it's not really my role to . . . Well, Brianna, I guess the best thing I can say to you is that I try to focus on today, on living my life to the fullest while I'm here, and let the future take care of itself."

Brianna smiled, told Leila thanks, but thought, Easy for you to say, lady.

a good person again

Josette in phlebotomy. Thank God. Josette was an artist, whereas stupid Kathy couldn't find a vein with a map and always left Brianna's arms bruised.

"How's that boyfriend of yours?" Josette asked as Brianna's blood flowed through the thin plastic tubing and into the first of several vials.

"He's not my boyfriend," Brianna said, smiling in spite of herself.

Josette eyed her critically. "Well," she said, "you're better off. Trust me."

Brianna laughed and wished Dr. Patel had half the bedside manner Josette did.

On to Dr. Patel, who praised her for doing so much better. She'd hated Dr. Patel ever since the beginning of summer, when she stood over Brianna's bed and told Dad, "Unfortunately, she's really taken a turn for the worse."

First of all, duh, she wouldn't be in the hospital with an oxygen hose up her nose if she hadn't taken a turn for the worse. But what had really hurt was the disappointed tone Dr. Patel had used. Like Brianna had really let her down. If she had been able to speak at that point, Brianna would have told Dr. Patel that she'd done everything right—well, almost everything. Anyway, she'd pretended she wasn't chronically ill and she'd kept a positive attitude, all that stuff that was supposed to keep you from dying, and it hadn't worked. It turned out Brianna's lungs hadn't cared about her attitude.

So Brianna had lain in the bed with a terrible attitude, an attitude that only got worse as the days stretched into weeks. Only Melissa and Stephanie had come to visit her every day, and all those other people, people like Brian or Cathy or Emma who would smile in her face and write stuff in her yearbook like "I'm always there 4U," turned out not to be there 4 her at all. She knew it was incredibly boring to be stuck in a hospital room, but only Melissa and Stephanie had gotten how their being bored for one hour made the other twenty-three bearable for her. It turned out that being popular was just about as useful when things got bad as a positive attitude. When you're at the very edge of existence, you've got only the lungs you were born with and the people who really love you, and everything else is i: i for illusion, i for the square root of negative one, an imaginary number. You can pretend it exists to solve certain problems, but the bottom line is that it's not real.

And yet, here Dr. Patel was praising her for doing better, and she couldn't help but be proud of herself. It was as if getting better was a decision Brianna had made, as if Dr. Patel were the teacher, and Brianna had studied really hard for the recovery test and gotten an A.

$$\infty$$

At home, Brianna flopped on the couch, hoping to make up some of the sleep she'd lost that morning.

She drifted in and out of consciousness until the dialogue on TV faded, and she sank gently into a nice nap.

Her phone yanked her back up into groggy consciousness. She looked at the screen. Ashley. Annoyed, she hit the button to silence the phone and rolled over on the couch.

Except now she couldn't sleep. Ashley hadn't visited in the hospital, of course—she couldn't put herself at risk like that—but she'd sent mail every day. Postcards or letters on Hello Kitty stationery. She always wrote the right thing, because who knew better what the right thing was than someone who'd been there? So instead of "You mean so much 2 me, we will B friends 4 Ever," Ashley had written stuff like "Went swimming in the lake today and swallowed so much gross water I ended up puking. Mom had a complete fit," and "I'm actually really nervous about starting at BHS, even though I know it's going to be a blast."

And Brianna had repaid her by ducking her. Why? She told herself it was just because Ashley was so much younger than she was, but that wasn't really it. No, the real reason she hadn't been calling Ashley was Molly. Because with Molly gone, that put Brianna in the Molly role and Ashley in the Brianna role, and if that was true, then Brianna would be following Molly into the ground.

She knew it was stupid. School was starting the next day, and she'd have to see Ashley in the hall, so she had to return the call. Ugh. Once I make this call, she thought, I'm back in it, back to being the CF mentor, back to trying to be brave to set a good example, back to feeling like I let Ashley down whenever I have a setback. She thought about how she would have felt if Molly had stopped calling her. Bad. She dialed Ashley's number. She felt guilty when she heard the delight in Ashley's voice.

"Oh my God, Bri, how are you?"

"Great. I just got back from seeing our pal Laxmi Patel."

"Everything okay?"

"Yeah, I needed the okay to get back to school, and of course a little pat on the head for doing well."

"I hate that," Ashley responded. "She acts like you're a puppy who learned a new trick if your numbers are good."

"Yeah," Brianna said, "or a puppy who peed on the rug if they're bad."

Ashley laughed. "Hey, so we had our freshperson orientation this morning."

Brianna remembered parading through the halls in small clusters, getting schedules, and feeling sick and terrified the whole time. "How scared were you?"

"I wasn't really that scared. I mean, I've heard so much about it from you that I . . . Yeah, okay, it was really scary."

"The good thing is after a week you'll be as bored and grumpy as the rest of us."

"I can't wait. Hey, can I ask you about my teachers? We got our schedules today."

"Sure." Brianna was enjoying this. As much as she didn't want to feel like Molly, it was kind of fun to be an expert.

"Okay. So for English I have Ms. Beekley?"

"She's nice, but hard. She makes you read a ton."

"That's all right. What about, uh, Ms. Kelemanik for math?"

"I don't know. She must be new."

"How about Mr. Sangermano for history?"

"He's really nice. But, you know, it's still history."

"I like history."

"Whatever floats your boat. What about science?"

"Stevenson?"

"I loved his class. He hates boys, so they always get called on and the girls always get good grades."

"Cool. I can use an easy A."

"Yeah, I think Stephanie got a B minus just for showing up in his class. Best grade she got all year. Of course I had to actually do the homework, but that plus showing up got me an A."

"Cool."

Brianna gave cafeteria advice, and locker-room advice, and homeroom advice. Ashley wanted to know what Brianna was going to wear for the first day, and Brianna stopped short, realizing that this was the first year she could remember that she'd given absolutely no thought to that question.

"I don't know. I guess jeans and a T-shirt or something. I honestly haven't thought about it."

"My mom promised to take me shopping tonight, so hopefully I can find something cute. Except I now have these very attractive dark circles under my eyes from not sleeping because of the new meds, so I'll have to find something that matches those," Ashley said.

"I've been there. I keep hoping they're gonna put me on something that gives me boobs, but no luck so far." Ashley laughed at this, and they said goodbye.

Well, Brianna thought, I'm a good person again. And it hadn't really been that hard. Except that she remembered calling Molly after orientation, and the way Molly had laughed, and her nasty sense of humor, and Brianna started to feel really, really sad. She quickly called Melissa, asking, "Hey, what are you wearing tomorrow?"

not like the others

School hadn't changed. The cafeteria floor still held its usual 8,040 blue-and-white linoleum squares, the door to the part where you got your food was still leaking foul smells, and, as always, there were a few kids eating those nasty muffins they sold in here in the morning. Brianna spotted her friends. Stephanie looked good even with her blond hair at shoulder length, the shortest Brianna had ever seen it. Melissa looked amazing with her long brown hair and her perfect body, flapping her hands around, her blue rubber bracelet wobbling on her arm as she did so. And then, Brianna thought, there's me, the stick figure who looks like a freshman. One of these things is not like the others . . . Brianna got to the table and found that Stephanie had, as usual, eaten all the chocolate Munchkins, so Brianna popped a powdered one in her mouth while Melissa had one of her typical freak-outs.

Melissa talked in between big gulps of coffee. "Somebody remind me why I'm taking pre-calc. I'm so nervous."

"So you can, quote, study something besides cosmetology and not end up like my mom, unquote," Stephanie said.

"Oh my God, Bri, promise you'll help me with math," Melissa said. "Please, it will wreck my college chances if I fail it."

"I don't know, Brianna might have her hands full, um, tutoring Todd," Stephanie said, smiling.

Suddenly Melissa grinned. "Tutoring? Is that what they call it now? What exactly did you make sure he learned?"

"Okay, Mel, what did *you* learn in your *lifeguard training* this summer? I've never really heard of anyone being resuscitated in quite that way before."

Melissa laughed. "Hey, he was breathing hard at the end, okay? Seriously, Brianna, please, I'll do anything, just promise me you'll help me with pre-calc so I can go to college."

Brianna shook her head and grinned at her friend. "Okay, but only if you can get this bitch to stop eating all the chocolate Munchkins."

The girls laughed. They watched as some dorky short guy in khakis and a tie seemed to wander their way.

"Who's that?" Stephanie asked.

"New teacher," Melissa replied confidently. "You can tell by the terror in his eyes."

"Why's he coming over here?" Stephanie wondered.

"I don't know," Brianna said. "But let's do the party trick."

Melissa and Stephanie nodded as the guy arrived at their table.

"Good morning! I'm Mr. Michaels, new in the English department, and I guess I'm on duty here this morning," the new teacher said, smiling. His smile seemed genuine.

Melissa and Stephanie mumbled good morning, not returning Mr. Michaels's smile.

"So, I just wanted you ladies to know that you dropped a couple of Munchkins on the floor there, and I wanted to make sure you pick them up before homeroom, because, if I can speak frankly for a moment, the lunch ladies here are terrifying, and they're going to take it out of my a—— um, hide if the caf is a mess after I'm on duty."

They laughed, because the lunch ladies really were mean, and because the guy had almost sworn on the first day of school.

"I'll just get those," Brianna said, and as she leaned over to pick up the glazed and jelly-filled Munchkins, she knocked her purse off the table with her elbow. The cheap magnetic clasp popped open as it always did when Brianna knocked her purse over. The contents spilled out onto the floor, and she bent down to start picking stuff up. She watched as a dime rolled about fifteen feet across the floor and wondered if there was any way to figure out how fast it would have to be moving in order for it to stay rolling on its edge. She didn't even know what the variables were—maybe she'd learn that in physics.

Mr. Michaels froze. Brianna knew she was being mean, but it was kind of funny watching him get flustered as he faced two bad choices—either stand there and watch her pick stuff up by herself or violate the sanctity of a teenage girl's purse. Finally he bent down and said, "Here, I'll give you a hand." Brianna kept glancing at Mr. Michaels as she pretended to fumble with change. He was unfazed by the tampon, but made no move to pick it up. She gathered the nearby change and picked up her phone. She saw Mr. Michaels furrow his brow a little bit, wondering if he should take it away as the rules said he should but nobody ever did. Then she saw the furrow get even deeper as he saw the cigarettes and Slimodex pills.

Brianna also saw Mr. Michaels taking her in—the small, undernourished body, the slight cough that escaped her mouth at that point—and looking back at the pills and cigarettes and deciding that this poor anorexic smoker was really ruining her health.

"Okay, well, I'll be on my way now. Nice to meet you all," Mr. Michaels said as he practically ran to the other side of the cafeteria.

They waited until he was a respectful distance away and then started laughing.

"He didn't even let us whisper how worried we are about you," Stephanie said.

"Yeah, I think we freaked him out," Brianna said. She tucked the two-year-old pack of cigarettes and unopened Slimodex pills back into her purse. She imagined what it would be like to be the girl she pretended to be—deeply screwed up and destroying her body instead of having it destroy itself. It didn't seem all that bad. Because if you were screwing up your own body, then at least you could stop.

They quickly got over the thrill of running the party trick on Mr. Michaels, and the conversation turned to college. Brianna didn't want to talk about college; actually, she didn't even want to listen to anyone else talk about college. She grabbed another Munchkin. If you assumed it was a perfect sphere, you could probably calculate the volume, which might be interesting, but not as interesting as calculating the surface area. Because then if you knew the size of one grain of powdered sugar, you could estimate how many grains of powdered sugar it took to cover the entire surface of the Munchkin.

She was so intent on the Munchkin that she didn't notice that Melissa and Stephanie had stopped talking. They were giggling, and when Brianna looked at them, their giggles turned to laughter.

"What are you calculating this time?" Stephanie asked.

She could tell them, but they'd only make fun of her. "How early I have to get here to get a freaking chocolate Munchkin," she said.

"Will you just get all chocolate next time?" Melissa said. "Why do you even do this? We always throw out the plain ones, but you keep getting the assortment."

"But if I get a box of chocolate Munchkins, I'll eat them," Stephanie replied.

"Yeah," Brianna said, "that's kind of the idea."

"For you, maybe, but some of us actually gain weight when we eat this stuff," Stephanie complained. If it was anybody else, Brianna would have bitten her head off, talking about how she'd trade a big butt for being able to breathe, but with Stephanie she merely rolled her eyes. Stephanie was tens of thousands of Munchkins away from being fat. In fact, if you gained a pound for every 3,500 extra calories you consumed, it might be possible to calculate how many Munchkins Stephanie would have to eat every day to get fat if you knew how many calories were in each one. Brianna might even go into Dunkin' Donuts and ask, because a scrawny teenage girl asking how many calories were in one Munchkin would make everybody there think she was anorexic.

"That's twisted," Brianna said.

"No," Melissa said, "I think the bear claws are twisted, not the Munchkins."

"Ha ha," Brianna said flatly. Stephanie punched Melissa in the arm.

"Mel, that was a sucky joke even for you," Stephanie said.

"Yeah, well, good thing I'm cute," Melissa retorted.

The bell rang, signaling the official start of the school day. Reluctantly, Brianna got up and faced the long march to homeroom. Lots of people smiled and waved, but since the crush was on in the halls, nobody really had time to stop and talk, which was good.

Jim, Mike, and Kendrick stood in the hallway. As girls walked by, they said either "Yes" or "No" really loud.

"Pelletier!" Jim called out. "We need a new nose tackle this year! You goin' out for the team?" This joke never got old to him. One way or another, he'd make it several times a football season. "Pelletier!" he'd holler. "We need you! Rico's out for the season!"

And Brianna, understanding that this was a gesture of affection, that it meant Jim thought of her differently than he thought of all the other girls, had never been annoyed by it before. Today, though, it just seemed tired. Yes, Jim, she wanted to say, it certainly is amusing that I am underweight due to my fatal condition. You know what else is funny? My pancreas doesn't function properly! And, get this—the tissues in my lungs are shot to hell! Yuk yuk! Instead she smiled politely and said, "Okay, Jim. See you at practice."

He laughed like this was the funniest thing he'd ever heard. Brianna turned away as some chubby goth girl she didn't know walked by in a black miniskirt and black tights around her very thick legs. "Oh, no!" Jim and Mike and Kendrick all said, then started laughing.

Brianna turned into homeroom and wondered if these guys, her friends, were always this dumb and cruel. Had they gotten worse, or had she just gotten a clue?

Ms. Vincent, looking bored and obviously calculating how many hours she had to continue teaching until she could finally retire—at 6 hours a day and 180 days a year, Brianna figured maybe

5,400 more hours—handed Brianna her schedule, saying without enthusiasm, "Welcome back. Any questions on your schedule need to go through guidance." Nice to see you, too, Brianna thought.

She looked at her classes. Brainiac math, normal everything else. She wondered how that would look to MIT if she did decide to humor Dad and go to their info session.

She guessed she'd probably look pretty good. She'd been getting letters and brochures from all kinds of engineering schools since she'd taken the SAT, and she knew she could squeeze out a killer "I'm a courageous kid with CF" essay without even really trying. If she wanted to.

That, not her grades or her course load, was the problem.

"Hey, Brianna," Adam Pennington said, "taking AP Calc?"

"Yeah," she answered. Adam was a nice guy, but he looked really young and didn't party or do sports, and Brianna was the only non-misfit she knew who would talk to him. They had been alphabetical-order and math buddies since the ninth grade, and they were always the ones who looked pretty much the same after every summer vacation. Except this September, Adam's face seemed to be clearing up, and, while he'd looked about thirteen last June, he now looked nearly sixteen.

"Have you heard about Eccles?" Adam asked.

"Heard what?"

"He was in a band!"

Brianna looked at Adam blankly. About fifteen percent of the senior class were in bands, and it wasn't really surprising to find that the calculus teacher who everybody said smoked enough weed to get the entire senior class high had once been in a band.

"I mean a real band! With records and groupies and everything. My cousin told me. There's even a Pearl Jam song about him."

"No, there isn't," Brianna said.

"Yeah, there is. I guess Eddie Vedder used to vacation here or something. I can't remember the song."

"Hmm. Well, I'm gonna have to stay skeptical."

"Dare me to ask him about it?"

"You mean in class?"

"Yeah, sure."

They sat in homeroom for another ten minutes while Ms. Vincent read something off of a piece of paper in a monotone voice and nobody listened, and then they all filed into the halls.

this castle of
marshmallow fluff

English looked tolerable, and history looked completely horrible, not to mention boring as hell, but at least she got to sit with Mel and Steph in those classes. They were in her gym class, too, but she decided she was probably going to have to get another "Special Circumstances" note to get out of it.

Finally, right before lunch, it was time for AP Calculus. Deciding she needed a boost if she was going to be able to concentrate, Brianna stood at her locker and washed a handful of Funyuns down with a swig of ice-blue Gatorade.

This made her the last one into class, but fortunately Mr. Eccles didn't seem to notice. He was a big fat guy with wild, wispy hair on the sides and almost no hair on the top. He was wearing a hideous red paisley shirt. Standing in the front of the room with a half smile and a big gut, he looked kind of like the Buddha statue next to the register at the Jade Garden restaurant.

"As surely everyone is aware," the teacher began, "one James Doubt graduated from this school and went on to great fame in the National Football League. Many is the student who hopes to follow in Mr. Doubt's footsteps. And yet, in the twenty-four years I have been a teacher here, approximately thirteen senior football players graduate each year, and of those, exactly one has achieved success in the National Football League, making the odds of success in that area—"

"About point three percent," Brianna found herself saying, because she'd reflexively started solving the problem. There was a pause. She caught a dirty look from Lisa Stiehm.

"Absolutely correct, Ms. . . ." Mr. Eccles said as he looked at his grade book.

"Brianna Pelletier," Brianna finished.

"Correct, Ms. Pelletier. Now, in the same time period, at least a hundred students have gone on to be engineers, doctors, scientists, and computer professionals due to their pursuit of mathematics.

"So your presence in this class shows that you understand the importance of mathematics to your future. But on your way to The College of Your Choice," Eccles continued, as Brianna winced, "we are going to ponder the infinite, tame the unknowable, imagine the unimaginable, and make sense of that which is senseless."

Brianna felt cold. Math gave her brain something to do *besides* pondering the infinite.

"Now, in any math class, we deal with facts. Fuzzy abstraction and uncertainty simply disappear in the reality of numbers. Correct?"

Brianna nodded. Exactly. Besides the fact that she was good at it, what she liked about math was that everything made sense. There was always an answer, even if it was hard to find, and you could prove it was right. It was like there was an itch in her brain that she could scratch by doing a math problem.

"I am sorry to inform you that the castle of mathematics that we've convinced you is a solid thing made of stone is actually a dreamlike structure made entirely of, say, Marshmallow Fluff."

Mr. Eccles pointed up at the number line on top of the blackboard. "Consider the number line, an imaginary line full of numbers, which are what? Simply ideas. You can have two *of* something, but can you ever hold the number two in your hand? No. But, as you know, the number line extends forever.

"And you also know that prime numbers, like integers, never stop. It's not as easy to find the next one, but there are always more. So there are an infinite number of prime numbers.

"Here, then, are two infinities. One is all integers. The second, only those integers that are prime. Which of these infinities is larger?"

The class was silent. It was kind of screwed up that you could have two different-sized infinities, even though you really couldn't. Mr. Eccles looked like he was going to wait for an answer, so Brianna raised her hand. "Ms. Pelletier?"

"The question doesn't make sense. Infinity is like forever, so infinity is just infinity. If neither one ever ends, they're the same, even if they're"—and here she paused because a lot of the snobs in this class were looking at her like she was nuts—"different."

"Yes!" Mr. Eccles yelled. "Infinity is infinity, and therefore all infinities are equal, even though some are, to paraphrase Mr. Orwell, clearly more equal than others.

"Now this is, as we said when I was your age, really freaky, man. It's very hard to make yourself think about it. But fortunately, we stand upon the shoulders of giants, and the ability of Leibniz and Newton to wrap their minds around things that are simply unimaginable to most of us brings us the calculus.

"It turns out that this discipline born of things imaginary and difficult to think about is very good at describing the world.

"Indeed, without this structure of abstractions, this castle of Marshmallow Fluff that is mathematics—and I do apologize, it is getting close to lunchtime, and I, too, feel pangs of hunger—we could never do something as concrete as lifting a 747 off the ground.

"Thus, you see, mastery of mathematics makes you incredibly powerful, for you become a concretizer of abstractions. Presented with ideas so foreign to our experience that they can only just barely be contemplated, the mathematician smiles and tames them with rules, indeed, brings order from chaos. Is this not, my friends, the very definition of creation? This is not simply an adventure, it is *the* central adventure of human existence, and I am pleased to be able to share it with you. Questions?" He smiled as he said this, knowing he had completely messed with their minds.

He'd messed with Brianna's, too, but in a good way. While all that infinity stuff did trouble her, she liked what he said about mastering it with math. It was exciting. Brianna knew most of these kids from her other math classes, and she suspected a bunch of them were probably pretty annoyed right now. Like the fat guy said, they liked math because it was real.

Brianna pictured the number line continuing forever in both directions, shooting off the edges of the earth, a tangent to the sphere. She was flying next to it through space, past the planets, just going and going and going, flying along the number line, counting integers and primes and never stopping.

Brianna zoomed back from space when she saw Adam raise his hand. She knew he was going to ask his dorky music question. She wanted to shake him. She was patient with Melissa and Todd and others who didn't get math like she did, but she got frustrated with how completely clueless Adam was about acting in a way that wouldn't make people want to punch him. She winced as Mr. Eccles called on him.

"A question, Mr. . . . ?"

"Pennington."

"Yes, Mr. Pennington. You wish to stump me with Zeno's paradox? I assure you that we will deal with, and hopefully dismiss, Zeno's paradox in time. Meanwhile, your homework for this evening is a simple review set of problems which you can find on page twenty-four of your textbook."

This was Mr. Eccles's way of saying not to ask him any questions, but Adam didn't get it. "Actually, I just wanted to know if you were really in a band. My cousin said you played bass for the Electric Prunes or something."

You could always get teachers off track by asking them something about themselves, and Brianna pondered the fact that if only Adam had the good sense to do that at the beginning of class someday, maybe after they'd already lost ten minutes to a fire drill, then people would actually like him for it. But he had to ask when they'd already been dismissed five minutes early for lunch.

"Mr. Pennington, I would *love* to discuss those days, but right now I believe the collective growl coming from your classmates' tummies would drown out my answer. My clue to you is fourteen."

All right, everyone, please depart from my sight and fill those rumbling bellies of yours."

As she stopped at the desk at the front of the room to pick up the textbook that looked like it weighed as much as she did, Brianna asked Mr. Eccles, who was pulling out what looked like a Fluffernutter from his drawer, "So what's Zeno's paradox?"

His face lit up. "Ms. Pelletier, you've delayed feeding your belly in order to feed your mind. Wonderful and admirable. As you can clearly see"—he patted his gigantic gut—"it has, unfortunately, been years since I did the same. And, indeed, I am quite hungry right now, so you will forgive me if I take a small bite of my sandwich . . ." He bit into the Fluffernutter, which made Brianna hungry. "Ahh, that's better. Now, Zeno posed to Socrates a paradox which I will now paraphrase. On your way to the cafeteria, you will, at some point, have traveled half of the distance to the cafeteria. Correct?"

"Um, sure."

"And from that halfway point, you will eventually reach a point half of the remaining distance to the cafeteria. And from that point, you will reach a point half of the remaining distance. And so on and so on, to infinity, actually. For if you continue to travel half the distance, you will, of course, never reach the cafeteria at all, but merely continue to cut the remaining distance in half forever.

"Thus Zeno appears to have proven that you can never reach the cafeteria from here, which is undoubtedly news to those of your classmates already standing amid the pungent smells of"—he rooted in his desk and pulled out a photocopied calendar with the lunch menu on it—"sloppy joes. With Tater Tots." He smiled. "It's quite easy to refute Zeno by simply walking to the cafeteria, but proving him wrong by means of mathematics is far trickier."

"Okay. Thanks!" Brianna said, suddenly feeling self-conscious that she was chatting with a teacher after class. She threw an embarrassed "See you tomorrow" over her shoulder, and bolted from the room.

In the cafeteria, Melissa and Stephanie were already eating. "Where were you?" Stephanie asked.

"Calc. Hey, when do we get to sign out for lunch?"

"Not till next week," Melissa replied.

"Too bad. I would kill you for a Fluffernutter," Brianna said.

Melissa laughed. "I love you too, Bri. Good to know I come second to a sandwich. Just out of curiosity, does widdle Bwi need the crusts cut off, or would a regular Fluffernutter do?"

"Shut up." Brianna sat down and contemplated her turkey and cheese sandwich. She took out the knife and the small Tupperware of mayo that Dad had packed. She cut the sandwich down the middle, then thought for a minute about telling Stephanie and Melissa that she could make this sandwich last forever, that if she could eat half the sandwich every day, she would never ever finish it. Then she thought better of it, spread the mayo, and started to eat.

it's gonna be fine

At the end of the day, Brianna hiked up to the third floor where the ninth-grade lockers were. She really just wanted to go home, but she felt like a good mentor would check in on her mentee. As she passed the door to the second floor, she thought she saw Todd down by the sophomore lockers. He had been up at his parents' camp in New Hampshire all summer, and she had no illusions that he was being faithful to her or anything, because they weren't really boyfriend-girlfriend, but she still thought he might have called when he got back. Then again, she hadn't called him.

Up on the third floor, she waded through the sea of short, loud boys punching each other and squealy, jittery girls hugging because it had been a whole forty-five minutes since they'd seen each other. Had she ever been like them?

Well, no. Most ninth-grade girls have the beginnings of an adult body, Brianna thought.

She found Ashley, who was also skinny but already sporting a

B-cup—how unfair was that?—at her locker with a couple of her friends.

"How was it?" Brianna asked.

"Hey, Brianna!" Ashley said. "It was cool, I guess. Oh, sorry, Bri, this is Sarah, Keri, and Caitlin."

"Hi," Brianna said, as she looked at three identical little blond girls she would never be able to tell apart.

"Do you need a ride home?" Brianna asked Ashley.

"Oh . . . well, my mom's picking us up," Ashley replied.

"Okay. Well, I gotta go—Melissa's probably panicking about pre-calc already, so I should probably calm her down," Brianna said, suddenly feeling stupid. She'd thought she was doing Ashley this big favor, but it turned out Ashley didn't need her at all.

Ashley didn't need her, but Melissa certainly did. Brianna's phone rang as she was walking down the stairs.

"Where are you?" Melissa sounded desperate.

"I'm heading downstairs. Where are you?"

"I'm waiting by your car."

"I'll be right there." When Brianna got to her car, Melissa hugged her and lost it.

"I should just drop out right now and go to Blaine and rent a chair next to my mom at the salon, because I'm going to fail math and not get into any college anywhere."

Brianna patted her back. "Okay, Mel, okay. You're not going to fail. I'll help you, it'll be fine."

"It's not gonna be fine! Oh my God, he was so mean . . . it was like I wandered into Chinese class or something. I completely didn't get it."

"We got you through Algebra 2, right?"

"Yeah."

"So we'll get through this, too."

"Okay."

"I need food, though. Let's go get a snack and look at your homework."

it's all math

Before school the next day, Melissa and Brianna had to hear again about how Stephanie was really going to dump Kevin this time, but at least Stephanie had had the good sense to buy all chocolate Munchkins. In homeroom, Adam came up to her and exclaimed, "Hey, Brianna, it's Love!"

People were looking over at them and smirking. Brianna wanted to crawl under the desk. "Um, what do you mean?"

"The band that Eccles was in! It's called Love. They were a sixties band. I've been doing research on these psychedelic bands: the Electric Prunes, the Strawberry Alarm Clock, the Chocolate Watchband, Moby Grape—"

"You're making this up, right?"

"I swear to God, they were real bands! Anyway, they've all had like a million people in them, but none of them seemed to be Mr. Eccles. But then I found this one called Love, and they have this big song called '7 and 7 Is.' "

"Um, yeah?"

"Remember when he told me my clue was fourteen? '7 and 7 Is'? Get it?"

"Well, okay, maybe."

"So I look at this Web site, and guess what the second guitarist's name is?"

"Eccles?"

"Yes! Well, sort of. I mean, they spelled it E-C-H-O-L-S, but I don't know if that was a mistake, or if he changed his name for the band or something. Dare me to ask him about it?"

"Well, if you want."

Adam started digging through his bag. "Here," he said, handing Brianna a CD. "I downloaded a bunch of Love songs for you." Adam blushed. "I mean, you know, songs by the band Love. I burned you a copy."

"Thanks, Adam," Brianna replied, smiling as she took the CD and put it into her bag. She wondered briefly if his making her a CD meant anything. She hoped not. He was her only ally in calc class, and she didn't want anything messing that up.

Brianna refined the timing of her walking and snacking and arrived in class two minutes early. She had a Fluffernutter in her bag because she'd been craving one so bad after yesterday that she'd called Dad at work to ask him to bring home Fluffernutter supplies.

Eccles went over the homework, and then started back in on the mind-blowing stuff. "Critical to our work in this class are quantities we shall refer to as infinitesimals. These are quantities which are infinitely small. Now what could I possibly mean by this?"

He waited for a hand to go up, but nobody budged. Nervous and uncomfortable, Brianna reached up to scratch the side of her head.

This, apparently, was a mistake. "Ms. Pelletier, as I know you only slightly, I don't know whether you were raising your hand or gathering steam for a head scratch, but, nonetheless, you can handle my question, yes?"

"Okay," she responded, and paused for a minute. She wanted to make sure she said exactly what she meant to say. She saw some of the other kids smirking, but she wasn't going to open her mouth until she had it right. Finally, she answered, "Well, between zero and one, there have to be an infinite number of points that match up to fractions where the denominator keeps getting bigger. So something like one over two times ten to the 500th or whatever is going to be really really small, almost zero."

"Yes, Ms. Pelletier, indeed. As the integers grow infinitely large, fractions grow infinitely small, and as we follow those fractions toward zero, we will reach a point so close to zero that it is, for many purposes, zero, except when we don't want it to be."

The rest of the class looked about as baffled by that as Brianna was.

Everyone was silent, and Eccles seemed to savor the confusion, and just as he was about to speak, Brianna felt that familiar tickle in her throat. She tried to fight it, but the tickle got worse and worse, and she had to let one cough out, one tiny little cough so small that most people probably wouldn't even register it. Unfortunately, letting that cough out led to more coughing, which led to more coughing, and pretty soon she was hunched over her desk, face red, knowing she had to go to the bathroom and hawk one into the sink. Still coughing, she got to her feet, looked at Eccles, who nodded, and left the room.

It took her another minute to stop coughing, and another couple to fight back the post-tussive emesis, which is what the doctors called it when she coughed so much she puked. She stood over the toilet for a minute, willing herself not to vomit. After getting it under control, she splashed some water on her face and went back to class.

Everybody was trying to solve a problem when she got back, so she took out her notebook and started working.

By the time class was almost over, when it was time to pack up and get to lunch, Adam did it again. His hand shot up, and Eccles sighed and said, "Mr. Pennington?"

"Did you play guitar in a band called Love?"

"Mr. Pennington, in my youth I did a number of regrettable things, and so there are several years for which I have only the foggiest memories. I certainly remember something about playing guitar, but beyond that, it is all somewhat of a purple haze." He grinned and said, "Don't forget your homework, which is on the board, and have a wonderful remainder of your day."

Adam was right next to Brianna as soon as she walked out of the classroom.

"It's totally him! Did you hear that?"

"Yeah, but it sounded inconclusive to me."

"I think he's just messing with me. You're not gonna forget being in a band like that."

"No, I guess not," Brianna conceded.

They walked in silence for a minute, and Adam, kind of randomly, busted out with, "I'm going to MIT next month for an interview and an info session."

"My dad's on my butt about going to one," Brianna told him.

Silence erupted again, and she couldn't stand it. "Is that where you want to go?"

"Absolutely," Adam responded, his face lighting up. "I really . . . well, no offense or anything, but I really hate Blackpool and Blackpool High. I'm going to throw an application in at Caltech and UC Berkeley, but I just want to go somewhere close with a bad football team where nobody calls you a fag and punches you for being smart."

Brianna looked at him and saw that he was blushing. He was keeping a straight face, but his voice had kind of cracked when he said that. "Oh," she said. "Um, is that a funny exaggeration?"

He looked at her like she was the stupidest person on earth. "No." His smile came back, and he said, "Anyway, you should go, even if it's just to get your dad off your back. Here," he said, digging a pen and a notebook out of his bag and scrawling a date and time on a piece of paper. "Here's when I'm going. Maybe I'll see you there." They finally reached the ground floor, where Adam added, "Though I think I'd stand a better chance at MIT if we had a normal teacher who just told us how to solve stuff that's on the AP and didn't try to mess with our minds all the time. That stuff about which infinity is bigger makes it harder."

"I dunno," Brianna said as they reached the cafeteria doors ("Take that, Zeno!" she thought), "I actually kind of like that stuff. Well, there's Steph and Mel." Though they were math and alphabetical-order buddies, Brianna and Adam inhabited very different places in the rigid social seating chart of the cafeteria.

"See you," Adam said. "Tell me what you think of the CD."

"I will!" Brianna watched as Pete, a football player Stephanie had hooked up with last year, bumped into Adam. She wondered if it was an accident.

As she sat down at the table, Melissa said, "Hey, Bri, your boyfriend's cute!" She and Stephanie laughed.

"You just never get tired of that joke, do you?" Brianna asked.

When she got up to throw her trash away twelve minutes later, she saw Mr. Eccles, on cafeteria duty, standing next to the garbage cans. The cans were nearly full, and Brianna placed her lunch bag gingerly on a spot where it looked like it might not topple the trash overflowing from the top.

"Ah," Eccles said, "sometimes I like thinking of the stacking of trash in the can as a function with an as-yet-undiscovered limit. I believe, Ms. Pelletier, that your bag has brought us an infinitesimal distance from the limit of this particular function. When Mr. Teague there arrives with his Mini Chips Ahoy wrapper, I think this particular function will become undefined."

"I guess we'll see," Brianna said. She coughed, thankfully only once, and then walked away, turning back only as she heard the sound of garbage falling on the floor. Jim Teague was standing there looking stupid, and Eccles was grinning. "It's all math!" he called out to her.

Brianna rolled her eyes, but, as she headed out of the cafeteria, she wondered if everything really was math, or if there were some things that couldn't be plotted or predicted.

you set the scene

After dinner on Sunday, the "so" Brianna had been waiting for finally came. "So," Dad said as he handed her a dish to dry. "Have you picked an MIT info session yet?"

Brianna sighed. "No."

Dad washed a pot in silence for a minute. "You told me you would."

"I know, I know."

"I need to be able to believe what you tell me, honey," Dad said, still looking only at the pot he was washing. Ugh. She hated that he was playing it this way. Instead of giving her all kinds of reasons why she should go that she could argue with, he was just pulling "I need to be able to trust you, that's the kind of relationship we have," which was his strongest card. She was always amazed at how Stephanie and Melissa pretended to be somebody for their parents that they really weren't, and as much as he got on her nerves, she was glad she never had to do that with Dad.

"Fine," she said. "I'll do it this week. I promise."

"Really?"

"Yes, okay! I promised. I don't break my promises."

"I know you don't," Dad said. "It's something I admire about you."

"Jeez, Dad, I said I would call, you don't have to keep laying it on so thick."

Dad stopped washing and looked at her. "I'm not blowing smoke up . . . I'm being straight with you, Bri. I want you to do something with your incredible brain, so you don't end up working at Bargain Zone. And I *do* admire you."

Brianna was about to respond, but Dad jumped in, "Not because of the CF, but because of the kind of person you are."

Brianna felt really uncomfortable. "Thanks," she said quietly, and stowed away everything she wanted to say about how even spending the time filling out applications to go to a college she'd never live to get a degree from was pointless. And how she had to stop preparing for things because there wasn't going to be a future to prepare for. It was actually a relief not to say any of that stuff, because as she turned it over in her mind, it felt scary.

Later, Dad was in the garage tinkering with his bike, and Brianna sat alone at the kitchen table with her homework spread out in front of her. It had been light out when she sat down, so the only light on in the house now was the one lonely light that hung over the table. She'd already done all the homework she didn't mind doing, and she'd talked to Stephanie once, and Melissa twice, though one of those calls was her talking Melissa through an easy pre-calc problem, so that really didn't count. She reached into her bag for her history book ("The Slab of Tedium," Melissa called it), and her hand found the CD Adam had given her.

She took it out of the case. "Love: Forever Changes" was scrawled on it. She put it into her CD player and slipped the earbuds into her ears. Even if it sucked, it would give her something to think about besides the incredibly boring history chapter she had to read.

The music was weird—it wasn't at all like anything she could place. She guessed it was rock because there were guitars, but there were a lot of trumpets and violins, too. The guy sang in this kind of fruity voice, and the lyrics reminded Brianna of "step into the freezer with Uncle Ebenezer" or whatever the crap was that the stoner kids always played at their parties, but then weird lines about people dying and blood coming out of the bathtub and people with snot caked on their clothes kept jumping out at her.

As she was finishing the questions on the chapter, she heard this:

For the time that I've been given's such a little while
And the things that I must do consist of more than
    style
There are places that I am going
This is the only thing that I am sure of
And that's all that lives is gonna die
And there'll always be some people here to wonder
    why
And for every happy hello, there will be goodbye.

The song went on and on. When it ended, Brianna hit the back button and listened to it again, pausing and backing it up as she came to the part about how short your time is.

This, she thought, is exactly why I don't want to apply to college. She had never been able to put it into words, but she felt something she realized was relief. Here was somebody singing—okay, in a weird song that she could never play for Stephanie or Melissa—something she'd been feeling but had been unable to put into words. She couldn't apply to college. There just wasn't enough time.

And on her third listen to the song ("You Set the Scene," Adam's chicken scratch on the jewel case insert told her), what struck her was the part about how there would be people left to wonder why, and she had this image of Dad standing over her grave and crying. Just for a minute, she thought that would be the absolute worst part about dying. First Mom broke his heart, and soon Brianna was going to break it again. As much as she hated being a burden to him, hated the sacrifices he made for her, she felt even worse about the idea of making him sad forever.

The CD ended, and Brianna sat there in the silence under the lonely light and cried.

i was thinking about you

Before she left the house on Monday, Brianna wrote a note that said "Call MIT" and taped it where she'd be sure to see it, on a bottle of Gatorade in the back of the fridge.

At school, she plopped down at a table and turned on her CD player. She'd woken up thinking about this weird music, and it was satisfying to hear it again—like eating a Fluffernutter after Mr. Eccles got her thinking about Fluffernutters.

She was only two minutes into the first song, "Alone Again Or" (Or What? Brianna wondered, but the song, which didn't even have the word "or" in it, gave no clues), when she saw Todd step into the caf. He obviously saw her, but he pretended he didn't. He performed an elaborate head-slapping show like he'd forgotten something, and walked out again.

She sighed as the guy on the CD said he'd be alone again tonight. Well, that was certainly it for Todd. It wasn't like he'd been some great love or anything; they had been friends, and they'd helped each other out. She made sure Todd didn't fail Algebra 2 for a second time; he made sure that she didn't die a virgin. Brianna had given Todd strategies to get through math at a C level, but she couldn't really make him get it on a deep level, and she certainly couldn't create in his brain even the palest shadow of her appreciation for the beauty of math. And Todd, for his part, hadn't been able to make Brianna understand what the big deal about sex was.

Still, she was able to check something off her "Things to Do Before I Die" checklist because of him, and they had been friends, or at least friendly enough that he wouldn't pull cheesy moves like pretending not to see her. Well, if that's how he was, she was better off without him, which was what Dad was always telling her anyway. Still, she felt like she knew what would happen next: he'd continue to pretend she didn't exist, then he'd be at his locker with some sophomore girl with big boobs who looked twenty, ostentatiously kissing her all the time and pretending that he'd never been with the senior girl who looked twelve.

She scrawled "Don't you dare come to my funeral, loser" on a piece of paper. She wondered if she should fold it up and put flower doodles on the outside and slip it into his locker like she had a couple of times when they'd arranged tutoring sessions.

She laughed to herself at the thought, but it started her coughing. Fortunately, it didn't last long, and she was able to pull what she hoped was a very discreet tissue-to-mouth-phlegm-spit maneuver. She didn't like the coughing, but she was used to it, and everybody understood. The spitting, though, never stopped being gross and embarrassing, but once she had seen what that stuff looked like on a tissue, there was no way she was going to swallow it.

She smiled, remembering Melissa's reply when she'd told her that. The CD played on, and Brianna found herself hoping that

Melissa and Stephanie would be late. She wanted a few more minutes with this weird music that her weird math teacher had made.

The music got her thinking about Molly, and then she did something really stupid. She reached into one of the many zipper pockets on her backpack and took out the envelope she had carried there for the last five months but hadn't looked at since last April. Just seeing Molly's handwriting on the outside of the envelope felt like an electric shock, and Brianna knew she might start bawling. Put it away, she told herself, look at it later.

But her hands kept going, opening the envelope and seeing Molly's note. Way too short. Way, way too short. Why didn't you write more, Molly? Why didn't you tell me something useful about how to do this?

> **Hey, girl! Looks like I'm on the homestretch here. I hope you'll read this poem at my funeral. I like it a lot. I love you and I'm sorry I have to go.**
>
> **Love,**
> **Molly**

Thirty-five words. Just under 1.7 words for every year Molly had lived. And then a photocopy of a poem by Robert Frost called "Good-by and Keep Cold" that Brianna had read a hundred times, that she read again now, that she couldn't really make sense of, except, "I have to be gone for a season or so." Now her tears were really about to come flooding out, but a tap on her shoulder snapped her back into the cafeteria.

She hastily stuffed the envelope into her backpack and looked at the tapper. Adam, smiling a big smile. She was relieved that somebody had pulled her out of Molly's funeral, but she was annoyed that it wasn't Stephanie or Melissa. Right time, wrong person.

"Did you get a chance to listen to the CD?" Adam asked.

"Yeah," Brianna said. "You know what? I really like it! I mean, it's kind of freaky. I don't know. I like the way it's kind of pretty and psycho at the same time."

Adam got a goofy, enthusiastic look on his face. "I'm totally there. I listened to it once and thought it was the weirdest piece of crap ever, but then I couldn't do anything else until I heard it again. I played it probably five times last night."

So it wasn't just her. That was a relief.

"I downloaded a bunch more songs from other albums if you'd like them," Adam said.

"Sure!" Brianna replied. Adam reached into his bag and pulled out a CD. He had printed the cover of some old Love album and put it in the jewel case; it was printed so small that Brianna couldn't make out much except that one of the guys was wearing flood pants and ankle boots. Which one was Eccles, thirty-five years and fifty pounds ago?

"I was really into the lyrics, so I downloaded all of them and printed them in the booklet," Adam said.

"Cool!" Brianna said with unfeigned enthusiasm. As she took the CD she saw Katie and Keianna, two of her "friends," watching her with Adam the geek and whispering and giggling. They went over and sat down with Chris and Jim, two more people Brianna would once have called friends, and she felt all four of them looking at her.

Brianna took the CD and put it in her bag and thought this semi-dorky guy had done more for her in the last two days than most of the people she'd once considered friends ever had.

"Thanks a lot, Adam," she said.

"Okay, well, I better go," Adam said, looking over her shoulder. "Bye!" he called as he practically ran away.

Stephanie arrived about one second later.

"Hey, Bri, how's your hot friend?" Stephanie said, grinning.

"Shut up. He's good."

"I saw his body language. I don't know, Bri, I think he likes you."

"He does not. We're math buddies, and he made me a CD and—"

"He made you a *CD*? And he doesn't like you? Yeah, okay."

"What are you talking about?"

"Making somebody a CD is a way of saying, 'I was thinking about you when I was home. Alone. In my *bedroom*. With a box of tissues and—' "

"Okay, okay, you're disgusting. Are you just trying to make me lose my appetite so you can have more chocolate Munchkins? 'Cause it's not gonna work."

Stephanie started talking about how Kevin was acting weird, and Brianna knew this meant there was breakup drama on the way.

to ponder the infinite

When Mr. Thompson, the college counselor, finally ended Thursday afternoon's senior class assembly at the final bell of the day, Brianna bolted out of the auditorium. She could hear Stephanie calling "Bri!" behind her, but she had to get out of there. She jumped into the Sunfire and putt-putted up the street, swinging the car around a corner without hitting the brake. It made her feel a little better, but still not good. She could go home, but today was Dad's day off, and she really didn't want to talk to anyone right then.

Her phone started playing those familiar notes in her purse—probably Stephanie or Melissa. It was definitely somebody who was planning to go to college, and probably somebody who wanted her math skills to help them out. She let the call go to voice mail.

Brianna drove until she reached the beach. The snack shack was shut for the winter even though it was still September, but Mario's House of Clams was open. She grabbed a Gatorade and her enzyme pills out of her bag and went in and got some fries. She poured a bunch of salt on them and walked over to the beach. She wondered idly what the volume of this strange french fry container was. It was a rectangular solid, but it sloped up from the bottom like a cone. So neither formula would really fit. One more thing in life that seemed simple but was actually really complex.

There was hardly anybody on the beach. It was a sunny day, but it was windy, and it was barely seventy degrees out. She sat in the sand and watched the waves and ate her fries. She tried hard not to think. Some guy came by with his golden retriever, and he chucked a stick into the freezing cold water and the dumb dog went right in after it. Brianna thought about how this simple act of a guy throwing a stick for his dog needed some pretty complicated math just to figure out how fast the stick might be going, or to describe the path it took into the water. It would be hard to account for that end-over-end thing the stick was doing. Describing the arc of a tennis ball would probably be easier.

Her phone rang again. She took it out of her purse and looked at the caller ID. Melissa. She'd call her later. She turned the phone off.

A cold breeze blew in off the waves, and Brianna was starting to wish she'd brought a sweatshirt. A plain sweatshirt, though— not a UMass or URI or Dartmouth, or BC, BU, or any of those other ones that everybody was wearing around school these days.

She couldn't believe that in the middle of the senior class assembly Mr. Thompson had said, "We are all facing challenges— whether you are battling a difficult situation at home, or cystic fibrosis, or muscular dystrophy—" and everybody had looked at Brianna and Keith Who Is in a Wheelchair. Then he went on about how every adult in the building was there to help them win their personal battle, or scale their own mountain, or something. Then he'd reminded everyone that now was the time that the college process started to get serious.

Brianna grabbed a rock from the sand and tried to throw it in an inverse parabola. She picked up another one and tried again. She did this for a long time. So long that she started to feel tired from the effort of throwing rocks, which got her depressed since she'd been throwing rocks to try to stop thinking. She thought of getting her CD player, but she didn't really need to: Love's songs were playing in her mind on what seemed to be an endless loop. Little bits of the album kept popping into her brain, as though it had become her personal soundtrack. Still, if she wanted to hear more than a few seconds of a song at a time, she'd need the CD. She threw another rock and decided to go back to the car and get it. Before she could even turn around, though, she heard a voice behind her. "Curves . . . acceleration . . . speed. The very heart and soul of the calculus, here . . . on our own . . . humble beach!"

It was Mr. Eccles, sitting on the sand. Everybody said he was at the beach every morning in the summer, but Brianna had never seen him before. It was kind of odd to run into a teacher out in the real world like this, especially when you were trying to get away from everybody.

His face was so red it was practically purple, and he was huffing and puffing like he'd just run there all the way from school. "Hey," she said. "Are you okay? You want some Gatorade or something? I haven't even opened it yet, so there isn't any backwash or anything."

"Ah, the magical concoction from the . . . University of . . . Florida. No, Ms. Pelletier, I can't take the . . . electrolytes . . . from your grasp . . ."

He looked awful, and Brianna wondered if she should call 911. This was weird, and embarrassing. She worried that if he passed out, she might have to give him mouth-to-mouth. She wondered if running to get Mario from the House of Clams to get him to do the CPR would cost Mr. Eccles his life and whether it would be worth it.

"Really, my dad gets these for like ten cents apiece at work, and I have another one in my bag." She held it out, thinking, Please don't keel over, old man, just take the Gatorade.

"Very well . . ." he said, taking the bottle and twisting the top open. "Your . . . intellect . . . is exceeded . . . only by your kindness."

"Um, do you want me to call somebody?" Brianna asked, hoping he'd ask her to call his wife or something and make this somebody else's problem. He shook his head no. He wasn't breathing as hard now.

So much for her time alone to think. But then again, that wasn't really working out too well anyway. She just wanted to call Melissa back and go home. But she didn't feel like she could leave her teacher sitting there. She felt awkward, so she picked up another rock and chucked it into the surf. She threw ten more rocks, pausing every now and then to cough and spit into the sea. Since Eccles was practically keeling over behind her, she figured he probably wouldn't be too scandalized by seeing her spit.

"Ms. Pelletier!" Mr. Eccles called out. Oh no. Now she was going to have to call 911.

"Um, yeah?"

"I want to express my gratitude for the beverage. Its revivifying powers were not exaggerated by the television advertising." He was smiling now, and looking a little bit less like he was going to croak. "I come here to ponder the infinite, and today I apparently almost touched it."

"I'm sorry. Are you sure you don't need a doctor or something?"

"Ms. Pelletier, I have seen enough of doctors to last a lifetime. They are tiresome even under the best of circumstances."

"I know what you mean," Brianna answered. Doctors *were* tiresome, but not nearly as much as social workers.

"So Ms. Carelli informs me," Mr. Eccles said. He'd obviously looked at her 504 plan and talked to the nurse. Even though it was a good teacher thing to do, she'd wanted to get some more of the school year under her belt before she became That Poor Girl. "I daresay you know better than I."

Brianna smiled. She liked the fact that he hadn't said anything about her battle or her courage. She decided she could chance making fun of him a little bit. "Indeed I do, sir, indeed I do." Eccles was getting to his feet, so Brianna felt like she could flee now, go home and see Dad and call Melissa.

Eccles laughed. "I do appreciate your kindness," he said. "I suppose I can now resume contemplating the infinite, though of course the ocean, despite its appearance from here, is not infinite."

"Okay then. See you tomorrow."

"Yes. It is looking increasingly likely that you will."

She hoped he'd be okay. He was a freak, but he was also kind of cool. For a second she thought about asking him what it had been like to be in a band, what he thought "Maybe the People Would Be the Times or Between Clark and Hilldale" was about, or telling him how much that record he'd played on was starting to mean to her. But that would be too embarrassing, so she started up her car and went home.

part of the music

When Brianna got home, Dad was sitting on the front steps talking to Cindy. Brianna closed her eyes briefly and tried to conjure up a stronger version of herself for Ashley's benefit. Because if Cindy was here, that meant that Ashley would be here, too.

She forced a welcoming smile onto her face. "Hi, Cindy! Where's Ashley?"

"Oh, I have to go pick her up from auditions. I was just passing through town on some errands and I saw your dad out here, so I stopped to say hi."

Brianna thought about that. They'd known Ashley and her family for five years, since they'd moved to town. They used to see them at CF picnics and stuff, back when Brianna would still let Dad do those things. And in those five years, they'd started to see Ashley's dad less and less. Maybe he was getting ready to bail. Or maybe Cindy had a thing for Dad. That "I just happened to be driving by" was one of Stephanie's signature stalking moves.

"Well, it's nice to see you," Brianna said, and started heading inside.

"Yes, I did get a lot done on my day off, and yes, I did mow the lawn. Thanks so much for asking!" Dad announced. Ugh. Brianna had thought she might escape the dreaded three questions since Dad was busy flirting with Cindy, but apparently not.

"I'm sorry, Dad. I just had a kind of bad day."

"So tell me three things about it," Dad said. He'd been doing this since middle school, after he'd gotten tired of her saying "good" whenever he asked how her day was.

"Okay, one, my math teacher just almost died on the beach. Two, you gave me an apple that was all bruise in my lunch. And three, Mr. Thompson is a dick."

"Brianna. Watch your mouth out on the street, please."

"Okay, if you watch yours when you're working on your bike and the garage door's open. What was it . . . something about the intake valve . . . I think the exact quote was 'Son of a motherf——' "

"Okay, okay. What happened to your math teacher?"

"I don't know. I went to the beach after school, and he was there huffing and puffing and I thought he was going to pass out. I gave him a Gatorade. He's a big fat guy."

"And why's Mr. Thompson a— Why don't you like him?"

"Dad, can we talk about it later?"

"When exactly?" Dad asked, smiling. "In the two seconds between when you hang up with Stephanie and Melissa calls?"

This comment was totally for Cindy's benefit. She was smiling the "it's so true" smile that pretty much everybody with a teenage kid did whenever someone made a joke like that. Brianna smiled in spite of herself. She decided she could talk about the CF part now in front of Cindy, who knew all about CF, and save the college part for later. Like never.

"Well, we had this senior assembly, and Mr. Thompson was talking about how they're all gonna help us climb every mountain or whatever, but he totally singled me out. He was like, whether you are battling a tough home life, or CF, or MD, we're here to help. I mean, I mostly felt bad for Keith, 'cause everybody was staring at him."

"That seems insensitive," Cindy said.

Dad got an "I need to protect my little girl" look in his eye. "He said 'battle'?"

"Dad, please don't. It's just . . . people are dumb, and lots of people—I mean even Leila at the hospital told me to keep fighting."

"I know, Bri. I'm not going to yell at him or anything, but I think we should have a little conversation so I can educate him."

"Dad, you would too yell at him. You're not calling him."

"Dammit, Bri, yes I am!" Dad was standing up now, and Cindy looked uncomfortable.

"No, Dad, you're not! I'm a legal adult, and I don't need you to protect me from every stupid thing, okay? You asked me how my day was, I told you the college counselor is a dick! You tell me all the time about how Mr. McCluskey at the store is a dick, but I don't call him up!"

She slammed the door behind her as she went into the house. She got some Oreos and a glass of milk and sat down at the kitchen table to start doing her homework. After twenty minutes of homework, she called Melissa back and told her she was okay, she was just pissed off. Melissa said that she and Stephanie went up to Mr. Thompson after and told him about how much Brianna hated the battle thing, and he was really nice about it and said he felt terrible and he owed her an apology. That made Brianna feel better.

She reached into the fridge for a Gatorade and saw her note to herself about calling MIT. She dug in her bag for the paper with Adam's info on it. If they went at the same time, at least she'd know somebody. She called and booked an interview, and the lady in the admissions office said, "Great! We look forward to seeing you there."

"Thanks a lot!" Brianna replied in her best fake-enthusiastic voice. She wondered if she could go into Cambridge by herself that day and tell Dad she'd been to MIT, and nobody would ever be the wiser. Except then she would have to lie to him.

But wasn't it a lie to get his hopes up about her going to college when she knew it wasn't going to happen?

Dad finally came in and was rattling around the kitchen, obviously wanting to talk to her. He rooted in the cabinet and pulled out two boxes of Hamburger Helper. "You want the cheeseburger mac or the stroganoff?" he asked.

"Cheeseburger mac," Brianna answered. "I called MIT."

"Great!" Dad responded enthusiastically.

He reached into the fridge for the ground beef. Head in the fridge, he added quietly, "I'm sorry. I won't call Mr. Thompson."

"Thanks. It looks like Melissa and Stephanie talked to him anyway."

Dad looked mad for a second. "So Melissa and Stephanie are allowed— Forget it."

Brianna bit her tongue even though she was annoyed. Another minute passed while Dad started browning the meat, and she started to feel bad.

"Hey, Dad," she said.

"Yeah?"

"I think Cindy wants you."

"Shut up, Bri."

"She does! What kind of errands does she have to do in West Blackpool? There's nothing here!"

"I dunno. You're too suspicious."

"Did she tell you about some problems she's having with Bill? That's what Stephanie does whenever she wants to break up with somebody. She goes to the new guy and is all 'You understand me, I don't know who else to talk to . . .' " Dad looked uncomfortable, and Brianna was really enjoying herself.

"She didn't . . . Well, I mean, she said . . ." he trailed off, and focused on stirring ground beef.

"I knew it! She's after you, Dad, I'm telling you, this is exactly how Stephanie operates!"

"I thought Stephanie got drunk and asked guys if they wanted to make out."

Brianna didn't know how Dad knew that, but she wasn't ready to concede the advantage just yet. "Oh my God, did she ask you to hook up? I'm going to kill her."

Dad turned purple. "Jesus Christ, Bri, of course she didn't, that's gross . . ."

He looked over at Brianna, who was smiling. "Gotcha," she said. "But seriously, how do you know about Stephanie?"

"It's a small house, and you don't exactly whisper."

Oh. That opened up a whole bunch of stuff that Dad might have overheard that he really wasn't supposed to know. Well, the best thing for that was just not to think about it and assume that the only thing he'd ever heard was her talking to Melissa about how Stephanie got when she was drunk.

After dinner Ashley called.

And Brianna had to admit to herself she was pleased. Ashley was about the only person besides Keith Who Is in a Wheelchair who could understand why she was upset about the assembly. And Keith Who Is in a Wheelchair was a big stoner, so conversations with him tended not to be that interesting.

She thought about telling Ashley about seeing Mr. Eccles on the beach pondering the infinite, but Ashley was so young and so positive that Brianna didn't want to drag Ashley into her own mess of fear and sadness.

Instead Brianna asked, "So how was the audition?"

"Whoa! How did you know I auditioned for the play today?"

"Your mom told me."

"That's weird. She didn't mention seeing you. But anyway, yeah, it was cool, I think my reading was really good, except I—I don't know—I coughed a little bit. I hope they don't hold that against me."

"I don't think they will."

"I mean, you'd hate to have your Juliet hack up a lung on stage. Not very romantic."

Brianna laughed. "Hey," she said, "do you want to go to the mall or something on Saturday?"

"Yeah!" Ashley sounded like she'd just won the lottery.

"Cool. I'll pick you up at ten-thirty?"

"Great!"

Ashley thanked Brianna, and Brianna said she had a lot of homework to do, so she had to go.

She was halfway through the most boring history chapter ever in the history of boring textbooks when Dad came in. He looked embarrassed.

"Hey, sweetie, I'm sorry to interrupt you while you're working."

"It's okay," Brianna said, but she didn't lift her head up, just so he would know to keep it quick.

"Well, if you're busy, we can do this later."

Brianna felt guilty almost immediately, and she wondered if that had been Dad's intention.

"I'm sorry, Dad, I just had to finish a paragraph. What is it?"

Dad had a notebook and a pencil in his hand, which was not something he usually carried. He also looked really uncomfortable. For a second she thought he was going to say something about how he and Cindy had been having a hot and heavy affair and Cindy was leaving Bill.

"So this guy came into the store today . . ." Dad paused, and Brianna wondered if he'd promised the guy a date with his beautiful stick figure of a daughter.

"And . . . he asked about my bike, and who had customized it, and when I told him I did, he asked if I would do one for him."

"Whoa, Dad, that's great! Congratulations!" Brianna was surprised he didn't look happier.

"Well, I kind of need some help figuring out what I should charge."

"Oh! Okay," Brianna said. She closed her history book, relieved to have some math to do. She made all the numbers really simple so it would be easy for Dad to do the math himself if she didn't make it until he finished the bike.

Not that she had any real reason to think that she wouldn't make it that long. It was just that Ashley reminded Brianna of herself in the ninth grade, and that felt like another lifetime, like that person she was in the ninth grade was dead already.

She didn't know if regular people ever felt this way or not. But she figured that if she did feel like something that happened three years ago was at the whole other end of her life, maybe she was steadily approaching her limit.

They kept telling her that people were living longer and longer, but she remembered lying in that hospital bed with Dad sitting there next to her and feeling like her lungs, and all the cells in her whole body, were telling her, "One more like this and you're on your own, kid, don't expect us to come along for the ride anymore."

She managed to push these thoughts away long enough to get her homework done and talk briefly to Stephanie. Stephanie was having more boyfriend drama, which distracted Brianna for a long time while she told Stephanie yeah, maybe if he makes you this unhappy, you should dump him.

Finally she went to bed. She tried not to think about anything, but it came back—that cold, hard fear in her stomach when she thought about being dead forever. She could joke about it most of the time, but when she really thought about it, it terrified her. She couldn't help thinking of being dead as just being all alone in the dark, and she wouldn't even be able to look forward to having it stop, and she would just spend forever like that, feeling sad and alone and scared. She felt like crying, and she wondered if she should wake up Dad. But he wouldn't have anything to tell her except whatever happens you won't be sick, which was okay, except it was better to be sick and have your dad and your friends around than to be unsick and dead and alone always.

She had to think about something else. She got up and popped the *Forever Changes* CD into her CD player. And for forty-two minutes, she felt better. She lay in the dark with the headphones on and the music playing, and she didn't have to think about being Brianna. She wasn't encased in a body that was lying on the bed; she was in the music. The CD ended, and, lying in the dark and the quiet, Brianna thought maybe being dead was like getting lost in music—maybe she'd just be lost in the music of the world, and she'd have no time to miss people or feel alone because she'd be part of everything. If you thought about it that way, it wasn't so very scary. She knew the terror would be back, but it was gone for tonight. She turned off the light and worked on her music fantasy, and pretty soon she was asleep.

really beautiful and horribly ugly

Brianna woke up and immediately felt the terror rising up again, but with Dad's weights clanking in the garage and the sky looking like it might contain sunlight sometime soon, she managed to focus on the day ahead and push her fear away.

When Dad was finished percussing, Brianna decided to tell him about that night. "So I'm sleeping at Melissa's tonight, okay?"

"Where's the party?"

"Dad, there's no party."

"Yes, there is. Where is it?"

"It's at Bryan McMahon's house, okay?"

"Who's driving?"

"We're walking."

Dad looked at her for a minute. "Really," he said in this flat voice.

"I swear! Bryan lives like two blocks from Melissa's house."

"And you'll remember all your meds?"

"Yes!"

"What about tomorrow morning? You gonna be home by five-thirty in the morning?"

"Dad, why did we even bother to train Melissa if you're going to ask me that every single time I spend the night over there?"

Dad looked at her again. "I want a call if there's any trouble or anybody needs a ride."

Brianna rolled her eyes. "There's not going to be any trouble, and we're not even driving."

"Okay. Just be careful, for God's sake."

"Dad, I'm always careful."

"And don't sleep with anybody who doesn't deserve you."

"Aaagh! You don't have to say that every time I go out!" Like anybody was even going to notice her, much less want to sleep with her if she was standing next to Melissa and Stephanie. They hadn't invented beer goggles powerful enough to make that happen.

"I know, I know, I just—"

"I know, you got drunk and did something dumb and you've been stuck with me ever since."

Dad's face turned red. "You know what? I tell you this stuff because I love you and I care about you. It's a really shitty thing to use that against me. Goodbye."

Dad stormed out of the house, started up his bike, and left. Well, the hell with him. Wasn't that why he was always telling her this stuff? "I got drunk and slept with somebody who didn't deserve me and got stuck with this CF kid and if you do the same, I might get stuck raising a CF grandkid, too, and I want to have a life when you finally croak."

It was pretty hard to hear about how those actions could have

unintended consequences when she was the unintended conse-
quence.

Brianna arrived at school feeling a mixture of barely sup-
pressed fear, annoyance with Dad, and dread of the awkward apology Mr. Thompson would offer if he saw her. She couldn't wait to
see Melissa and Stephanie, but she didn't want to talk about anything.

Melissa and Stephanie had their own problems. Melissa had a
quiz that day and was panicking. It took Brianna ten solid minutes
before she was confident that Melissa understood the concepts
enough to get through the quiz on her own.

As soon as Melissa's pre-calc problems were squared away, it
was back to Stephanie and how she and Kevin had a fight and then
he went to the mall with some girl from Gloucester named Kandy.
With a K. And she was actually asking *whether* she should dump
him.

"Steph, that's one strike and you're out," Melissa said.

"I know, but then he called me like an hour later and told me he
was sorry and he loved me—he *loves* me! He never said that before!
And he just sounded so cute, I mean he was really really sorry. And
it's not like I haven't gotten mad at him and called somebody else."

"Yeah, but . . ." was all that Brianna got out.

At that point the bell rang, and Melissa and Brianna just
looked at each other. "What are we going to do with her?" Brianna
thought at Melissa, and Melissa's look said exactly the same thing.

Adam had earbuds in his ears and yanked them out when he
saw Brianna walk into homeroom. "Hey."

"What's up?"

"I am completely obsessed with *Forever Changes*. I have no idea what most of these songs are about, but . . . it's just so cool."

"Yeah. I like it, too. Even if I don't understand it," Brianna agreed.

"You know what I get from it? Well, I mean, I couldn't really tell you what any single song is actually about, but I think the album is about how life is really beautiful and horribly ugly at the same time."

Well, Brianna thought, that about sums it up. She was silent for a second as she let Adam's words sink in. She'd been wondering what it was about the music that spoke to her, and that was it. It felt good to have somebody finally put into words what she'd been trying to figure out.

"Yeah, that's exactly what it's like," she said.

"Well, let's hope Mrs. Marrs buys it. I'm writing about it for English."

Brianna smiled. Here was another difference between her and Adam. There was no way she would ever write about Love for English class, or even tell anybody else but Adam about the CD. It felt too private somehow. Or maybe, she thought, she just didn't have the guts to admit in public that she liked something so weird. "You gonna, like, interview Eccles about it or something?" she asked.

"Maybe after my paper is done. I think it'll wreck my thesis if he tells me something about how they were all just stoned out of their minds and wrote words on pieces of paper and assembled them randomly or something."

Brianna laughed. "So I got an interview at MIT on the same day as you," she said.

"Cool! I'm glad . . . I mean, it'll be good to know somebody there."

∞

In calc, Eccles was fine, totally his normal self. You'd never guess that he'd looked like he was going to croak on the beach the day before. He gave the homework, and while everybody was packing up he called out, "Ms. Pelletier! May I speak to you for a moment please?"

Brianna felt nervous, like maybe she'd screwed something up in her homework, or, worse yet, that Eccles was going to bring up what happened on the beach.

"Yes?" she said, standing at the desk, books in hand.

"Ms. Pelletier, I believe I owe you one of these," Eccles said, reaching into his drawer and pulling out a Gatorade. Original flavor. Well, it was the thought that counted. "I do appreciate your kindness, and I would hate to see you wanting for a revivifying beverage."

Brianna took the bottle. "Thanks." She turned to walk out of the classroom, but then, on her way out, she said, "Hey, Adam made me a copy of your CD *Forever Changes*. It's kind of cool."

Eccles smiled. "Well, I certainly can't take credit for any but the most minuscule contribution to that album. I was merely a foot soldier executing the orders of a general who was a brilliant, if troubled, artist. Still, I'm always happy when that particular underrated masterpiece finds a new audience."

She didn't know exactly what she wanted to get out of talking to Eccles about the album. Maybe she thought somebody who made music about the beauty and horror of life would understand her more than somebody who didn't. Her curiosity about the album fought with her embarrassment about seeming like a dorky fan. "Um, can I ask you something?"

"Of course, though if it concerns the lyrics of that album, I must warn you that the only times I've felt I fully understood it, my thinking was somewhat . . . occluded."

"No, it's not that, I just wondered, when you go to the beach to think about infinity, what do you think about?"

"Well, Ms. Pelletier, there are times when I watch the waves roll in, and I think about all the waves that have crashed on this beach for hundreds of thousands of years. I consider the waves that will continue to crash against this shore for years and years and years to come. Sometimes just having this visual aid helps me to get my brain to deal with the concept of infinity."

"You mean like every wave is an integer or something?"

"Or something. Or perhaps every wave is a point between zero and one."

Suddenly Brianna felt awkward and wanted to go to lunch. "Okay, well, thanks."

She got about two steps, but Eccles kept talking like he hadn't even heard her say anything.

"And sometimes I sit there late at night or early in the morning, and I think about the vastness of the ocean, of the sky, of the spaces between us and the nearest stars, about the incredible, unfathomable bigness of it all."

Brianna could feel the terror curling around in her brain, and it never usually did that in the daytime. Why had she even brought this up? She really needed to get out of here, but Eccles wouldn't stop talking.

"And yes, it strikes me that in comparison to all of the humans on earth, to all the stars, to all the atoms in the universe, I am infinitesimally small. If we were to assign a number to all the atoms on earth—let's use the number one—my personal collection of atoms is so close to zero as to be nearly indistinguishable from zero. I mean, I am really not sure I'd want to divide by me."

Brianna's stomach was sour and panicky. Why wouldn't he shut up?

"But here, Ms. Pelletier, is the thing. Without infinitesimals, the calculus as we know and love it simply doesn't exist. It is these nearly-zero, sort-of-zero, sometimes-zero quantities that allow us to understand the world through mathematics. Something which seems to be nearly nothing turns out to be crucial to everything. So though I, or you for that matter, or any of us, may be, as a collection of atoms, practically indistinguishable from zero, this does not necessarily mean we are insignificant. Indeed, it may be that, like the infinitesimals in our discipline here, we are actually crucially important."

Brianna found herself cracking a smile. "I like that."

"So do I, Ms. Pelletier. Enjoy your lunch."

At lunch, Melissa and Stephanie were talking about something, but Brianna had a hard time paying attention. She kept thinking about being an important infinitesimal. It was a really good way to look at things, but the only problem was that she couldn't just wait for somebody to plug her into an equation and try to divide by her. She'd have to figure out for herself what this particular infinitesimal was good for.

a high-percentile family

After school, Brianna dropped the Sunfire off at home and squeezed into the backseat of Melissa's Echo.

When they got to the party, everyone was there. Although Brianna felt a lot farther away from all these people than she had the last time she'd gone to a party, which was in the spring, it was just nice to be in a house filled with people who were happy, to not have to do anything but just be there and be happy.

Even the fact that guys were buzzing around Melissa like bees did to that honeysuckle bush near the beach in the summer didn't bother Brianna. Since any of the guys with a brain, which was about half of them, knew that the best friend's opinion could make or break the deal, they went out of their way to engage Brianna in the conversation. She actually got a kick out of watching guys try to pull off this elaborate social maneuver where they showed that they liked Brianna but preferred Melissa.

Before Brianna had even reached the bottom of her first and only foamy beer from the keg, Stephanie and Kevin started screaming at each other. He called her a stupid bitch and she ran

off crying. Brianna locked eyes with Melissa, and they went into
rescue mode.

They grabbed Stephanie, who'd managed to get completely
trashed in the time it had taken Brianna to drink what she estimated was seventy-eight percent of the beer in a twelve-ounce cup,
or about 9.3 ounces, except that the cup had had about an inch of
foam in it, which threw her calculations completely out the window. Math was so much easier than the real world.

They pulled Stephanie out of the room while three or four
guys, at least two of whom were Stephanie's exes, started beating
on Kevin, and three or four of Kevin's friends started beating on
them. As they left the house, they passed Bryan McMahon on the
cordless phone in his front yard calling the cops on his own party.

Stephanie had gone from blubbering to the occasional whim-
per, and then she started saying stuff like "Hope he gets his ass
kicked." Somebody had to tell Stephanie the truth, but Brianna
didn't feel like she could, because she suddenly couldn't stand the
idea of Steph being mad at her. She tried shooting looks at Melissa
to tell her to just forget it, tonight was too precious to waste on a
fight that wouldn't change Stephanie anyway. She thought Melissa
got her mental messages, but Melissa said, "Steph, aren't you tired
of this bullshit yet? 'Cause we are."

Brianna didn't even hear Stephanie's response. Possibly thanks
to the beer, or the fact that something that seemed fun had been
interrupted by something violent and sad and gross, the fear had
crept out of the back of Brianna's brain and into the front again.

I'm leaving the party early, Brianna thought, and the fact that
I'm gone won't stop the party from going on. Mel, Steph, will you
two still think about me when you and your husbands are fat and

you drive your four kids to soccer and gymnastics in a minivan? Will you ever even think about me being dead? Will you think every time you have a birthday, every time you're with a new guy, every kid you have, will you think, here's one more thing poor Bri never got to do? Will you? Or will you just get on with life and say oh well, I'll see her when I get there? But you'll have other best friends by then. You'll have moms from playgroup, you'll have co-workers, and you'll be so old, so much older than I ever get to be, and you'll say I knew this girl once, and she died. Her picture's in the yearbook in the attic. You guys are the best friends I'll ever have in my whole life, you'll never be less than that to me, and I'm on my way to being just somebody you used to know, that poor girl.

When Melissa said, "Right, Bri?" Brianna told Stephanie: "Steph, I love you and you are better than this. And Melissa loves you and she knows you're better than this, too. It's not that we're tired of mopping you up because we have better things to do, it's because we love you and we hate seeing you in a puddle."

Stephanie whispered, "Thank you," and they all hugged in the middle of the sidewalk, until some moron driving by leaned out the window and yelled, "Hot! Give her a kiss!"

Back at Melissa's house, Brianna called Dad. "Dad, I need a ride," she said, and hoped that she wasn't making him climb off Cindy. Who knew what he did when she was out?

"On my way. Where are you?" Dad asked. Brianna told him, and they hung up. She had to give it to Dad, he was totally serious about that call-for-a-ride, no-questions-asked business. Brianna guessed that only some tiny percentage of parents who said the same thing would actually give you a ride without asking any questions. Probably less than five percent. Which put Dad in the ninety-fifth percentile of parents. Which put him only a few per-centiles down from where Brianna always scored on her math tests. We Pelletiers are a high-percentile family, she thought. What are the odds, anyway, of hooking up with somebody and getting a kid with CF from ten minutes in someone's room with the coats? Long, long odds. She wondered briefly whether they were better or worse than her odds of living to be thirty. Long, long odds.

Dad was covered in grease and dirt. He'd obviously been work-ing on that custom bike, and not Cindy. He put a dirty hand on her shoulder as he was driving. It was his way of saying he was glad she called, and he loved her and all of that stuff, and Brianna sud-denly felt about five years old. She started to cry.

"What's the matter?" Dad asked.

"I'm scared, Daddy," Brianna said, and once she named it, it was too much. "I don't wanna die. I'm so scared, I'm so scared."

Dad pulled the car over, and when she looked at him, she saw that his eyes were all wet, too. "I know, sweetie. I'm so sorry." He wrapped his arms around her as best he could.

They sat there for a while, with Brianna sobbing and Dad's eyes leaking. Finally he said, "So, it's only ten. You want some ice cream?"

"Definitely," Brianna replied.

As they drove toward Hot Licks, which was open till midnight, they passed the houses by the beach. One had a light on on the screen porch, and Brianna thought she saw Eccles there, sitting in a rocking chair. Contemplating infinity, she wondered, or just con-templating why you're all alone on Friday night?

it's lonely

The next morning, after Dad had gone to work, Brianna put *Forever Changes* on the boom box in the living room. She sat on the couch, closed her eyes, and listened. For just a few minutes, she was able to turn her mind off and get caught up in the music.

She put the CD on repeat, but for some reason it didn't work the second time. It was only eight o'clock, so she couldn't even call anyone to distract her. She got out her weekend homework and did it all, because even the Slab of Tedium was preferable to contemplating death.

At ten-thirty, Brianna hopped into the Sunfire and drove over to Ashley's house. When she rang the bell, Cindy answered.

"Hi, Brianna," she said. Cindy didn't invite Brianna in or tell her Ashley was in her room or anything. She just stood there quietly for a minute. Oh God, Brianna thought, she's going to ask me if she has a chance with Dad. She was certainly used to people asking her if they had a chance with Melissa or Stephanie, but Ashley's married mom would be too weird, too awful.

"I'm sorry," Cindy said. "Ashley's upstairs. Ash!" She yelled toward the stairs but got no answer. "She's probably got headphones on. Come on in."

Finally Cindy moved aside, and as Brianna walked by Cindy did that fish-out-of-water thing where she opened her mouth like she was about to say something, but no words came out. Brianna scooted up the stairs as quickly as possible and found Ashley in her room, listening to her iPod.

She had a flash of jealousy—having CF would probably suck less if you had all kinds of cool toys like Ashley had—but she pushed it away.

Ashley smiled and ripped the earbuds out of her ears when she saw Brianna. "Hey!" she said. "I am so glad you're here!" She hopped off the bed and quietly shut her bedroom door. "Mom's acting really strange today. I think she's gearing up for a meaningful talk, and I just want to shop. You know?"

Brianna didn't know what it was like to have the money to actually go shopping in the sense of going out and coming home with bags full of stuff, but she certainly knew about wanting to get out of the house and do something fun and brainless when your parent decided they needed to talk about something. Yeah, she knew that pretty well.

"Great," Brianna replied. "Let's do it, then."

They all but ran down the stairs, and Ashley yelled out "Bye Mom!" as they flew out the door and into the relative safety of the Sunfire.

At the mall, they spent a long time going from store to store, trying on outfits (and Brianna always had a reason why she couldn't buy anything—doesn't fit right, looks more like Melissa, just isn't for me). There probably weren't too many other ninth graders she'd like to hang out with, but she did enjoy hanging out with Ashley. And it wasn't because they could talk about CF stuff—it was that they didn't have to talk about CF stuff. Stephanie and Melissa couldn't keep that flicker of worry off their faces whenever she coughed, and they were nice to ask about all the meds and be understanding when she got tired and stuff, but Ashley just knew.

Eventually they decided it was lunchtime. Ashley wanted to go to Chili's. "Um, can we go to the food court?" Brianna asked. Here was the awkward part. Ashley didn't know what it was like to have a dad who worked at Bargain Zone and have no money for anything beyond gas and insurance. "I've only got seven bucks."

"I guess I owe you cab fare, so I'll pay you back with lunch," Ashley offered.

Brianna felt awkward about it, but not awkward enough to say no. After all, life was short, especially hers, and anything at Chili's was better than the four-dollar styrofoam plate of greasy lo mein she was going to have to get at the food court.

They got seated, and their waitress was this girl Kelly from calc class. "Hi, Brianna!" she said.

"Hey," Brianna said, smiling. Odd that they never greeted each other this enthusiastically in school.

"Oh my God, have you done that problem set yet?"

Yes, Brianna thought, I did it early this morning when I was trying not to think about death. She opted for a lie that sounded cooler. "Nah, I never look at weekend homework till Sunday afternoon."

"It's completely impossible. I think maybe Eccles was high when he assigned it."

Everybody was always talking about how Eccles was this big

stoner, and he certainly seemed to hint that it was true. And probably everybody who had anything to do with *Forever Changes* must have been high. (Is that another reason why I like that album so much? Brianna wondered. Is being sick somehow like being high?) He'd seemed to be having a lot of trouble breathing on the beach the other day. Maybe too much weed was his problem.

Brianna hadn't found the math homework all that hard. "Well, I'll be digging into it tomorrow afternoon if you want to call me."

"That would be great!" Kelly said, and she pulled her phone out of her apron and took Brianna's number. Brianna wondered idly if Kelly would ever call. Even though she was working at Chili's, she was East Blackpool all the way, and she'd probably have a private tutor or something. Brianna estimated the probability of Kelly calling her at about forty percent.

They ordered their food. Brianna got the chicken fajitas and felt guilty about how much they cost, so she just had water to drink. They talked about who Ashley thought was cute, how boring history was, and why the MCAS, which Ashley would need to pass next year in order to get a diploma, wasn't really that big a deal even though every teacher tried to scare you about it all the time.

Their conversation stalled out briefly, and Brianna noticed Ashley doing that same fish-out-of-water thing that her mom had been doing earlier.

"I think my mom and dad are going to get divorced," she said.

"Whoa," Brianna said. "Why?"

"I don't know. My dad's hardly ever around, and whenever he is, they're fighting. It really sucks."

"Jeez, I'm sorry." Brianna knew she was supposed to say something about how Ashley should know that if her folks did split up, it had nothing to do with her, but she knew it probably did. Which reminded her of Mom, which was not a subject she wanted to get into right then. But she had to say something. "I was too young to remember my parents fighting."

"I'm sorry," Ashley said. "I didn't . . . I mean, I just wanted to tell somebody who knew the whole thing, you know."

"Yeah," Brianna said.

"I'm really glad I have you to talk to," Ashley added. "It helps a lot. I mean, it's pretty impossible not to feel like a freak at school, even though everybody's wicked nice about it all the time, but it's lonely, you know?"

"Yeah," Brianna said quietly. "I do."

to talk to somebody

On Sundays, Brianna and Dad got to sleep late. The Bargain Zone people thought it was important for their employees to spend Sunday morning at the worship service of their choice. As long as said worship service allowed them to be at work by noon, or, if you were assistant manager and had to open on Sunday morning, eleven. What this meant for Brianna was sleeping until eight-thirty, which felt amazing, and going out to breakfast. Halfway through his breakfast (western omelet, home fries, wheat toast), Dad put his fork down and said to Brianna, who was chewing on the second of her three enormous blueberry pancakes, "So."

Well, here it was. He hadn't asked any questions on Friday night, he hadn't asked anything on Saturday, but here, finally, was the question that accompanied the no-questions-asked ride. Brianna steeled herself and replied through clenched teeth, "Yeah?"

"I'm worried about you, sweetie. I know you don't want to go back to group, but do you think it would help to talk to somebody?"

Whoa. This was a curveball. It wasn't about the ride at all. Dad had been true to his word. Which meant that Brianna was going to have to be true to her word about going to the MIT thing. "Well, I talk to Melissa, and Stephanie, and Ashley—"

"I know, honey, but I mean somebody who understands the stuff you're dealing with, and someone you don't have to be strong for. I know you hate the social worker at the hospital, but I talked to Dr. Patel, and there are all kinds of resources—"

"You talked to Dr. Patel?"

"Well, yeah, sweetie. Like I said, I'm concerned about you."

"She's not allowed to tell you anything! I'm an adult and my medical information is confidential!" The truth was that Brianna had authorized Dr. Patel to tell Dad anything, and she had filled out all the paperwork making Dad responsible for her medical decisions if she couldn't make her own. She knew she was being stupid, but she hated the idea of people talking about her behind her back.

Dad rolled his eyes. "Bri, I just asked her for some names of people I could call."

"Well, thanks, Dad, but I don't want to talk to anybody."

"It's your decision, of course. I just wanted you to know that you have the option. You're carrying so much right now, and you don't need to carry it by yourself."

Brianna softened somewhat, even though she was still annoyed. Sunday breakfast really was the worship service of her choice, and she hated to have it ruined by thinking about therapy. She sulked through the rest of breakfast and got sadder and sadder, and it wasn't until after Dad left for work and she was alone in the house that she realized why she was so sad.

"I wanna talk to Molly," she said aloud to the empty house. "She's the one I want to talk to. Nobody else. Just Molly."

She put on the other Love CD Adam had given her, which she hadn't even listened to yet because she'd been so obsessed with *Forever Changes*. She had an idea. She grabbed her notebook from history and turned to a blank page.

Dear Molly, she wrote.

How's death treating you? I miss you a lot, but I guess I'll probably see you soon, ha ha.

For the next hour, Brianna wrote to Molly about everything that she would have told her if she could call her up. It was hard at first, but it got easier, because in a weird way, it felt like Molly was alive in her mind while she was writing, and it felt good to talk to her.

When she finished, she realized the CD was over and she hadn't listened to it at all. She played it again while she folded her laundry, and it was disappointing. It wasn't bad or anything, and there was a song about waking up dead that she kind of liked, but it sounded a lot more normal than *Forever Changes*, and it didn't seem to be about her life the way the other stuff was.

Finally it was late enough to call Melissa. She was the only seasonal employee who seemed to be able to keep her job at Hot Licks during the school year, and she had to work all afternoon. "But you should totally come hang out," she said. "I'll give you free ice cream."

"Toppings?"

"Two dry toppings or one wet. None of this hot fudge *and* Reese's cups *and* Heath bars business."

Brianna smiled. "Okay. Deal."

She spent the rest of Sunday at Hot Licks. It was boring, but it beat being home alone.

the joy of the tater tot

Monday morning, Brianna saw Stephanie talking to Melissa and looking very happy and animated. Melissa shot Brianna a "Here she goes again" look, and Brianna prepared to bite her tongue.

Which she did as Stephanie described how Tom, one of the guys who had beaten up Kevin at the party, called her on Sunday night. "He was really sweet! He said he just wanted to check and see if I was okay. Isn't that nice?"

"It is," Brianna said. She had to tread carefully so she neither pissed Stephanie off nor betrayed herself.

"We talked for over an hour, and I think we're going to go out next weekend. It was really nice the way he stuck up for me, you know?"

"It is nice when people stick up for you," Brianna said. Well, that was true. Even if they were meatheads trying to beat the snot out of somebody.

∞

In homeroom, she started a conversation with Adam instead of letting him do it. "So I listened to the other Love CD," she told him.

"And?"

"Well, I have to say—I mean, it was okay, but it didn't grab me the way the other one did."

"I know. I really like '7 and 7 Is,' though. Hey, can I show you something?"

"Sure."

Adam dug into his bookbag and pulled out a paper. "Blood and Snot: Images of Ruin and Decay in Love's *Forever Changes*," it said on the cover page.

"It's my paper for English. Since you're the only other person I know who's ever even heard of the album, do you think you could read this and tell me if I'm completely insane?"

"Well, okay, but I'm more of a math person, you know."

"Yeah, me too. That's why I'm freaking out about this." Brianna looked at Adam for a second. If he was in AP English, he had to be good at it.

"Well, there's only a couple of minutes left in homeroom, so I can't read it now," Brianna said.

"It's not due till Friday; you can keep that copy."

"Okay then." Brianna tucked the paper into her bag. "Can I ask you something?"

"Of course."

"Aren't you . . . I don't know. I mean, I haven't told anybody about being into that record, 'cause it's so weird, you know, and I just . . . Aren't you worried about kids in your class making fun of you?"

Adam looked at her like she had three heads. "They make fun

of me anyway. I might as well get made fun of for being myself. I tried fitting in for a while—it didn't take. And then I just felt stupid for trying to be something I'm not and failing. No, I'm afraid this"—he pointed to his chest—"is the Pennington package, and people pretty much have to take it or leave it as is."

Brianna stared at him, and his face turned red.

"There's a really dirty package joke in there, isn't there?" Adam asked, grinning.

Brianna giggled. "I guess so."

"Well, I think I'll refrain from making any jokes about my package. Not that it's inherently humorous or anything . . ."

"Okay, okay, that's more than enough," Brianna said, laughing. Fortunately, the bell rang at that point.

The rest of the week was strange. Dad was working all the time. The guy who had hired Dad to customize his bike had sent a couple of other customers his way after stopping by to check on Dad's progress, and now Dad's cell phone was ringing constantly and there was barely room in the garage for his weights with tools and motorcycle parts scattered everywhere.

Brianna liked seeing Dad happy, and she was glad that he had something to occupy his mind besides hassling her about MIT. But seeing him this happy made her think she was holding him back. If it weren't for the cost of the meds and hospitalizations, he might be able to customize bikes for a living and tell Bargain Zone to take their assistant manager job and the health insurance that went with it and stick it someplace dark and tight.

School was completely normal. Mostly. History was boring,

calc and physics were interesting, and English was somewhere in the middle. Melissa was stressing about math and BU. Stephanie was talking to Tom every night and giving them the details. Brianna told Adam which parts of his paper were confusing, and he kept producing new drafts for her to look at.

And everybody, not just Melissa, seemed to be talking about college. Adam was always going on about MIT, and every teacher seemed to be talking about how you'll need this or that to get into college.

Ashley was caught up in the whirlwind of ninth grade and seemed to be having a good time, though she had called Brianna a couple of times at night close to tears because her parents were fighting again.

Despite the CF and her many absences, Brianna had always felt like she was part of everything at school. This week, however, she was starting to feel like school was a river flowing to the sea that was college, and she was on the banks, watching.

On Friday, Brianna was spaced when calculus class ended, so she was the last one leaving the classroom. As she walked past Eccles's desk, he said, "Ms. Pelletier?"

She looked up, surprised.

"Forgive me for the intrusion, but you haven't seemed yourself the last few days."

Well, she thought, I'm certainly not the self I was last year. I seem to be becoming a new self. She hadn't thought it was noticeable. Nobody else had said anything, but Steph and Melissa had their own problems. And so, for that matter, did Adam, who she guessed was her friend, too.

"I'm sorry," she said, "I just . . ."

"Oh, Ms. Pelletier, I'm not scolding you. I'm merely expressing concern."

"Well, thanks."

Eccles smiled. "Anytime." And Brianna noticed, approvingly, that he didn't offer to be someone she could talk to about what was bothering her, nor did he suggest that she needed to see somebody to talk about her problems.

Brianna moved toward the door, then stopped and turned around. Well, he seemed cool. After all, he'd helped make the album that seemed to be the only thing that helped her feel better right now, and he was also the only person who'd ever said anything about infinity (and death, which was the same thing) that didn't terrify her. Maybe she could tell him the truth. "It's just . . . Well, forget it."

"Yes, Ms. Pelletier? Is something amiss?"

Brianna said quietly, "I guess I'd like it if you didn't talk about college all the time."

"Ah. Is the application process bringing stress and heartache?"

"No, it's not that. I know you can get college credit for this class, but that's not why I'm taking it. I just like math. And I'm probably not going to college because . . . well, not to be too dramatic, but I guess I just . . . I don't feel like it really makes sense for me to make any long-term plans."

Eccles nodded. "Well, Ms. Pelletier, as you may have guessed from our encounter on the beach, long-term thinking doesn't make much sense for me either. And yet, if I could, I would most certainly spend my remaining time in college." She tried hard not to roll her eyes. She could feel Dad's favorite lecture coming: use the gift of your great mind, blah blah. But then, strangely, that wasn't what he said at all. "For if today's popular culture is to be believed, college life consists of a perpetual bacchanalia, a hedonistic dance of decadence not seen since the fall of Rome. In what other environment can young people constantly celebrate the fact that they possess adult bodies but no adult responsibilities? Indeed, it would seem, if my colleagues are typical adults, that this celebration of the seven deadly sins is the whole point of college for many people, that they go to college and engage in Dionysian revels so that they will have something to talk about when they become insufferably dull adults. Having settled into the unthinking somnambulism that passes for life for too many people, they look back fondly on their college years as a way of reminding themselves that once, if only for a few short years, they were actually alive."

Brianna looked at him, and, for the first time that week, she started to laugh. "That's certainly an argument my dad hasn't used. I guess I'll have to think about that one."

"Ponder it well, Ms. Pelletier. My advice to you is: get thee to a dormitory."

"Okay, thanks . . . Is it really true what you said about not thinking long-term?"

"I have some cardiac issues. There was a minor incident over the summer. According to my doctors, I need to make some significant lifestyle changes if I wish to avoid a major and possibly fatal incident. I've done some research, and, well, for a man of my age with heart problems, it seems time will be relatively short even if I do muster the willpower to make some lifestyle changes."

She looked at him. He'd said this with the same kind of tired resignation Dad would use if he said he had to work a double shift. Could he really be that calm about it? "Are you scared?"

He didn't say anything for a minute, and Brianna immediately felt embarrassed. She shouldn't have asked. But who else could she ask? Everybody she knew was probably scared of dying, but none of them were as close to it as she was. Or Eccles was.

"Yes. I'm scared. And yet, having devoted my life to a discipline that is all about imagining the unimaginable, I like to think about becoming one of those unimaginable mysteries. Sometimes when I'm telling a class about the infinite number of points on the number line between zero and one, I think this: One—not just the number one, but one of anything, the distance between any two integers on the number line, or a single orange, or a single human being—contains infinity. Do you see? Though I am but one, I contain the infinite. While you couldn't, of course, do this in practice, in theory it is possible to divide me an infinite number of times. I mean, if you could divide me by the infinite number of points I occupy, rather than by the finite, but ever-increasing"—he patted his gut—"number of atoms that make up my body. Thus, my hope is that, in death, I shall not cease to be, I shall just become more fully what I already am: one, and infinite."

Brianna found it comforting that maybe what was coming wasn't as different and strange as she'd been thinking. "I like that. Maybe one day I'll understand exactly how the sets of integers and primes can both be infinite," she said hopefully.

"Maybe, Ms. Pelletier, you will dance in eternity with the primes. You know, there has been a historical debate in mathematics as to whether mathematical concepts are created or simply discovered. In a discipline that exists only in the mind, how can anything be discovered? And yet it is the very usefulness of calculus in measuring, describing, and predicting the world around us that makes me think it was discovered, rather than created. It's pretty thin gruel when you really have to think about your life ending, but I do try to cling to the idea that even as some of these concepts describe our physical world very neatly, they may well provide some clues about what awaits us both, and, indeed, awaits us all."

They were both silent for a moment. Brianna smiled. "Kinda hard to think about lunch after something like that."

"Strangely, Ms. Pelletier, I disagree. For whatever joys the afterlife holds, I am fairly certain that the Fluffernutter is not among them. Thus, pondering the infinite reminds me of this fleeting, ephemeral joy that I should savor while I can." He dipped into his desk drawer.

"Well, I will then go savor the joy of the Tater Tot," Brianna said. "Thanks."

"Anytime, Ms. Pelletier, anytime. I will make an effort not to stress college so much in the future."

"Thanks."

"The least I can do. Enjoy your Tater Tots."

"Savor your Fluffernutter while you can."

"I plan to, Ms. Pelletier, I plan to."

Brianna walked down to the cafeteria feeling lighter than she had in a long time.

leave it alone

After dinner a couple of weeks later, Dad asked, "Can I get your help with this?" He pulled a computer box and a printer from the closet.

"Whoa, Dad! How'd you afford that?"

Dad smiled. "Well, I got a big advance from another bike customer, and with my employee discount, this was only four hundred bucks, so it's not that bad. But I'm gonna need to keep some records—you know, what I buy from who, who owes me money, this kind of stuff. So far I just have this"—he pulled out a cheap spiral notebook—"and I'm starting to get confused. I'd like to be able to give my customers an invoice that looks professional."

Brianna looked at Dad, standing there in a sleeveless T-shirt with some splatters on it from the sauce he'd heated up for their spaghetti dinner and his bike tinkering jeans, which had grease and dirt all over them, and smiled. A month ago, the idea of Dad saying he was concerned about professionalism would have been bizarre, and even now it didn't seem to fit with the person standing in front of her.

"Okay. Let's get started." They managed to get the computer turned on, and Brianna got Minesweeper running, but once they got into trying to set up a spreadsheet for Dad's new business, they hit a wall. Brianna knew that he was expecting her to be some computer whiz just because she was younger than him, but she had only ever typed her papers on Stephanie's or Melissa's computer. She knew somebody who did know computers, though. They turned the computer off and Dad washed the dishes while Brianna dried. Maybe because Brianna's mind was wandering back to infinity, or perhaps because she was afraid that one of Dad's "so's" was coming, she said, "Hey, can I ask you something?"

"Sure," Dad answered, squirting Bargain Zone–brand dishwashing liquid onto a sponge.

"Do you ever wonder what you're here for, or why your life matters, or anything like that?"

Dad handed her a wet plate and looked at her for a minute.

"What?" Brianna said, wiping the plate.

"Well," he replied as he pulled the saucepan out of the sudsy water that filled the sink, "I guess that's not a problem I ever have. I've known for eighteen years what my purpose in life is. I have to say that's one thing I haven't worried about since you were born."

Brianna felt stunned. She certainly knew that Dad made a lot of sacrifices for her, but she'd never really thought that he might think she was his whole reason for being alive. That felt heavy. And also, what would that mean for him when she died? What would his purpose be then?

"But if you're thinking about this stuff, I really don't want you to go the having-a-kid route. Not until you're older, anyway."

"Jesus, Dad, I'm not going to go get knocked up just so I can feel like I have a purpose in life!" Not like I could even if I wanted to, she thought. Her extra-thick mucus made her fertility unlikely, though Dr. Patel was always careful to tell her that this didn't mean she should have unprotected sex.

Dad smiled. "I know, honey. But a lot of people do. A *lot* of people."

Brianna dried, and chewed on that for a minute. "I guess that explains cousin Brittany, huh?" she said, laughing.

Dad laughed, too. "You know, I love my sisters, but yes, I think that explains pretty much all of your cousins." He paused. "On both sides, actually."

"I was thinking something more along the lines of a Nobel prize or something," Brianna said.

"Do they give those out for dish drying? Because if they do, I think you're taking yourself out of the running. There's a freakin' *puddle* in the cabinet there," Dad said, pointing to where she'd put away the improperly dried plates.

Brianna smiled and blotted the puddle. She thought about trying to steer the conversation back to the deep question of what her life was going to mean, but it felt good to laugh, and she decided to leave it alone.

let's start this up

In homeroom, Brianna asked Adam, "Do you know anything about spreadsheets? Like how to set one up?"

"Absolutely," Adam responded. Somehow she'd known that he was going to say yes. "I've got all my magic items from my Everqu—— Yeah, I've used spreadsheets before."

"Would you explain it to me? My dad is starting his own business and I'm trying to help him set up one of these things."

"Oh sure! How about after school?"

"Great," Brianna said, and then realized if Adam came over, Dad would tease her and she'd say no, we're just friends, and Dad wouldn't believe her. "I'll meet you in the computer lab."

"All right. Those computers are ancient, probably five or six years old, but I guess they'll do. The principles are pretty much the same."

"Okay! See you then." This didn't really count as social, but it would be the first time she'd ever hung out with Adam outside of class or homeroom. She hoped it wouldn't be awkward, especially since she was committed to be at MIT for the interview and info session at the same time as him.

After school, Brianna found her way to the computer lab to reserve a computer. It turned out she didn't need to, since there were only two other people there. She guessed pretty much everybody but her had a computer at home. And, come to think of it, even West Blackpool trash like her actually did have a computer at home now.

Adam arrived and sat down. "I can't believe they're still running Windows 2000. Well, like I said, it's all pretty much the same as far as the spreadsheets go, but I mean, wow. This is some really old stuff here. Okay, let's start this up . . ."

As Adam was clicking, Brianna's phone rang. Melissa. "Hey, Mel," she said.

"Help me. Please help me. I'm freaking out. Again."

"Okay. I'm up in the computer lab. I'll be done here in . . ." she looked at Adam.

"I give you my fifteen-minute guarantee," Adam said, smiling.

"Fifteen minutes."

"I'll be right there," Melissa said as she hung up.

"Okay," Adam said, and he began explaining how to set up a spreadsheet. Brianna took notes and was glad that Adam was able to explain things so clearly.

She was bent over her notebook and scribbling away when she felt a hand on her shoulder. She jumped and spun her head around. It was Melissa, who laughed.

"I told you I was coming," Melissa said.

"Yeah, I know. You just startled me. Oh, Melissa, you remember Adam. He's helping me with some computer stuff."

"Hey," Melissa said. Adam said hi. It was the first time Brianna hadn't seen him dumbstruck by Melissa's presence.

"I'm sorry," Melissa said. "I knew I was going to get home and freak out, and I just need you to help me understand this stuff so I can at least start my homework before I call you in a panic." She was pulling out her notebook and opening it, and Brianna realized Adam was waiting to finish doing her a favor.

"I'm sorry, Mel, I just, I asked Adam to help me with this thing, and we just need about ten min——"

"It's totally cool," Adam said. Brianna looked at him.

"Are you sure?" she said.

"Definitely. I mean, you know, Kirsten Dunst—well, she likes me to call her Kiki—doesn't usually call until four, so I'm all set as long as I get home by then. She gets jealous, you know."

Brianna laughed.

"I thought she was with some musician," Melissa said.

"Yeah, well," Adam said, "she *was.*" He gave this self-satisfied smile and took out a book.

Brianna was only about a minute into her explanation of Melissa's pre-calc homework when her phone rang. Stephanie.

"Hey, Steph, I gotta call you b——"

"Are you still at school? I gotta make up a math quiz in ten minutes, and I really need to ask you something."

"Computer room."

"Where?"

"Third floor."

"Be right there."

Brianna was just getting into the explanation groove when Stephanie arrived.

"I have a quiz," she announced, "and I am totally lost—this whole slope of a line thing."

"Take a number!" Melissa said.

"Hey, it's Bri's alphabetical-order buddy!" Stephanie said when she spotted Adam. For just a second, Brianna felt like she could look through Adam's eyes and into his brain, but his gross fantasies didn't interest her.

"Good afternoon," Adam said, bowing slightly.

"Hey, Adam, maybe you could do slope of a line with Stephanie while I do cosines over here," Brianna suggested.

"Happy to help," he said, obviously not quite able to keep his eyes away from Stephanie's chest.

Stephanie pulled a chair up just a little too close to Adam. Why did she do stuff like that? She wasn't really trying to flirt with him—to say he wasn't her type was like saying Brianna was occasionally a little bit under the weather—but it seemed that she just couldn't help it.

"I mean," Adam added, "I don't think Kiki will mind. What she doesn't know won't hurt her, right?"

"Who's Kiki?" Stephanie asked. "Is she your girlfriend?"

"Well, she *thinks* so," Adam said. "But, you know, she's getting a little clingy. I'm thinkin' I might have to cut her loose."

Melissa and Brianna cracked up.

Ten minutes later, Stephanie and Melissa were ready to face their respective math challenges, and not long after that, Brianna thought she knew enough about spreadsheets to help Dad put his together.

"Well, thanks," Brianna said.

"Anytime," Adam said. Brianna half expected him to add that this was the most time he'd ever spent with girls this hot, but then again, he didn't have to.

a chance in hell

Brianna had gotten the spreadsheet set up for Dad, but he still had questions, so over the next few weeks, she kept having to ask Adam stuff. He was always nice about it and explained everything really clearly. "Maybe I'll get myself a custom bike," he said on Wednesday. "I'm learning a lot about the nuts and bolts of the business, so to speak, and I think the bike might really match my bad-boy image. Not to mention the tattoo."

"You have a tattoo?" Brianna asked flatly.

"Well, not yet. I'm still in talks with the artist. I can't decide between a flaming skull on my chest or just the permanent eyeliner so I can get that Captain Jack Sparrow look."

Brianna thought it would take a lot more than eyeliner to get Adam to look like Johnny Depp, but she didn't say anything.

On Thursday morning, Brianna bit Stephanie's head off about nothing while they were having Munchkins, and when Adam walked into homeroom she actually felt her fists clenching. "Ready for that MIT info session?" Adam asked.

No wonder she was so tense. She had forgotten about it, but

obviously she'd remembered it on some level because it was making her grumpy.

"Yeah," Brianna sighed. "I'll be there."

"Cool," Adam said.

"Isn't the session happening right when Kiki usually calls?"

Adam smiled. "Kiki's so last week. Now I got Jessica Alba stalking me. I wouldn't be surprised if she shows up just to keep an eye on me."

"I don't know, Adam, you and these possessive girls."

"They know a good thing when they see it," he said, and just for a second, Brianna thought she could see his smile turning into a grimace, as though the pain of all his dateless years was trying to leak out.

∞

After school Brianna hopped in the Sunfire and began the drive to Cambridge. It wasn't until she got to the tollbooths at the end of the bridge that she realized she'd been too busy thinking about the interview and info session to think about driving off the edge.

She sat in traffic for what seemed like forever, and when she got to the campus, she drove around for fifteen minutes looking at the little map they'd sent her and trying to find a place to park. She seriously thought about bailing—between the traffic and the lack of parking in the whole godforsaken city of Cambridge, it was clear that she just wasn't meant to get there today. But she could picture the look on Dad's face when she told him, "I drove all the way to Cambridge and bailed because I couldn't find parking." Yeah, that wasn't going to play.

∞

The info session began in a conference room.

There were about fifteen kids sitting around a table, and some woman from the admissions office at the head of the table. Adam was sitting right next to the admissions lady. He gave Brianna a little wave. She nodded her head at him and sat in the only empty seat, next to a girl whose name tag said "Chiquita."

Brianna didn't know how to feel as she listened to a guy named Zach talk about student life at MIT. On the one hand, she had to admit that it was kind of exciting to think about just being somewhere where she could totally focus on what she was good at. It would be like taking only the parts of school that she liked.

Except for the people she liked. Melissa would be across the river at BU and might as well be a hundred miles from here. Stephanie would be at UMass–Dartmouth or Salem State if she was lucky, North Shore Community College if she wasn't. Brianna would be here with Adam. Maybe not everybody who went here was like him, but it hardly sounded like the fall of the Roman Empire party that Eccles had talked about.

The admissions lady—her name was Chia-Wen—started talking. "Of course, the advantages of an MIT education don't stop when you leave here. Our graduates have the highest starting income of any in the greater Boston area. You become part of an alumni network that includes major players in the top research universities and the top companies in software, biotech, and pretty much any other technical field you can think of."

Here we go again, Brianna thought. In high school, everyone's always talking about college. And apparently in college, everyone talks about life after college.

It was time for the tour, and they filed out of the room. "The guys aren't much to look at, huh?" Brianna whispered to Chiquita.

Chiquita looked around and smiled. "Yeah, it's a pretty sorry selection. But when I've got my biotech job and my six-figure salary, I'll have options my communications major friends won't even be able to dream of."

Brianna laughed, even though she was jealous. It must be nice to be able to take the long view like that. As the tour went on, Brianna started listening to snatches of conversation as people walked by. ". . . too much attention to the signal," a tall guy was saying to a short girl, "when the real action was in the noise!" They both laughed. "The whole time I was using the wrong coefficient!" an Indian guy was saying to a white guy. It seemed like everybody was talking about math, and she could tell by the looks on people's faces that they really loved it. In spite of the stuff about job prospects, this was a place where she would be able to immerse herself in math. Her brain felt the way it felt when she did a puzzle or solved an equation: buzzing, contented, good.

Her imagination strained at the end of its leash, and for the first time in months, she let it run free. She pictured herself as a student here, wearing a maroon sweatshirt with white letters and thinking about problem sets and physics, surrounded by smart people. She imagined staying up late and eating bad food and sleeping in a dorm and making friends and having all the guys she knew bugging her about when Melissa was coming over again.

Brianna was so caught up in her reverie that when the tour

ended and Adam asked, "Hey, do you want to grab some coffee after our interviews?" she told him sure without even thinking about
it, because grabbing coffee at five in the afternoon was the kind of
thing that cool college students did. Still buzzing with excitement,
Brianna sailed through her interview, rhapsodizing about the
beauty of math in a way that would have made Eccles proud.

It was only after she sat down with Adam that Brianna began
to regret her decision to have coffee with him. After they'd talked
about the tour and their interviews for about five minutes, there
was an uncomfortable silence.

"Um," Adam said, "listen, I've been wanting to ask you something."

Brianna wanted to smack herself on the forehead. Idiot! He'd
asked her to coffee so he could reveal that he liked her. Who would
she talk to in homeroom? Who would be her ally in calc class?

"Yeah?" Brianna said.

"Well, I . . . God, this is so embarrassing . . . I guess I was just
wondering if you thought I might have a chance in hell with
Stephanie."

Brianna really wanted to laugh with relief that it wasn't her after all, that they could still be friends. But she couldn't laugh, because he'd think she was laughing at the idea of him having a
chance with Stephanie. Which was pretty laughable, but it would
be mean to laugh.

It would also be mean to say the first thing she thought, which
was, "Maybe if she forgets her contacts and you have a bottle of
tequila," but she wasn't sure if that was meaner about Adam or
Stephanie.

"Hmmmm . . ." she said, stalling. Because how do you tell a guy no, you don't have a prayer, without hurting his feelings?

Uh-oh. Too late. Adam was looking at the table like it was the most interesting thing on earth. "I know, I know, it's ridiculous. Just forget I said anything, she's not really—"

"Well, here's the thing," Brianna said. "I wish she would go out with you, because she's a really good friend, and she deserves somebody as nice as you." Adam looked up with a hopeful expression on his face. "But right now, I mean, she seems to only be interested in guys who are stupid and treat her like dirt. And you're not dumb and you'd probably be nice to her, and I wish for both of your sakes that that was what Stephanie wanted, but right now it's not."

Adam was obviously happy that Brianna had said some nice things about him, but he still looked embarrassed that he'd shared his impossible dream and found that it was, in fact, impossible.

"I mean, have you seen the guys she goes out with?"

"Size and IQ of oak trees," Adam said with a wan smile on his face.

"Pretty much."

"Yeah. Well," Adam said. "Her loss, I guess." His face looked sad for a second, but then he recovered, forced a smile, and added, "I've always got Jessica Alba as a fallback."

"That skank?"

"Hey, I know she's not much to look at, but she has an inner beauty."

Brianna smiled, and they silently polished off their coffees. "Well, look, Dad's expecting me for dinner, so I should head out. You want a ride?"

Traffic was nightmarish, and for a while they listened to the music: Love's *Forever Changes*. They didn't talk, they just listened. She was glad they had this album in common, especially because listening to it was a lot easier than the conversation they'd just had.

no hassling me

When Brianna got home, just because she was kind of annoyed at Dad for being right, she decided to make him wait. He lasted five whole minutes before saying, "So."

"Yeah?" Brianna answered casually as she grabbed plates and glasses to put on the table.

"So, how was it?"

"It was good. I'm going to apply. But it's the only place I'm applying, no safety school, and no hassling me about the application."

Dad was trying to be cool, but he couldn't keep this gigantic grin off his face. "I'm really proud of you, sweetie," he said.

Now Brianna was the one who couldn't stop herself from smiling. She said, "Okay, okay, none of that. Everything's going to stay normal around here, all right? And don't start bragging about me or anything because I might not get in."

"You'll get in."

"Not if you keep jinxing it!"

"Okay. So do I get to hear about MIT, or is it all shrouded in mystery?"

Brianna found that she kind of wanted to talk about it, to tell Dad everything about the signal-to-noise guy and the campus and her sweatshirt fantasy, but she was too afraid that if she did say it out loud, if she dared to hope for life after graduation, she'd immediately fall sick.

"I know this sounds totally weird, but I just can't really talk about it right now. I'm sorry. It was cool and I'm going to apply, and I will talk about it later, but not yet."

"Okay. Do you have any recommendations yet?"

"Dad, that actually counts as hassling me about the application."

Dad held up his hands in surrender. "All right. I'm not hassling. So guess what I found in the break room today?"

"I don't know. Porno mags?"

"Worse. Webcam and mike."

"They're *spying* on you?"

"Well, not anymore. I just happened to trip over Joanne's purse that she'd carelessly left on the floor, which sent my coffee flying, and I'm afraid it might have gotten on some of the electronics."

Brianna laughed. "Good for you," she said.

"Total accident!" Dad said, pointing to the light over the table like it held a microphone and smiling. "I would never intentionally sabotage the property of the Bargain Zone Corporation!"

After dinner, Brianna called Melissa and Stephanie and did her homework. When she finally turned off her desk lamp and got into her pajamas, she realized she didn't hear the TV, and the sounds of classic rock coming from the garage must mean that Dad was still out there working on customizing somebody's bike.

to be kind to
our fellow creatures

The next week was November 8, Brianna's nineteenth birthday. She hadn't made plans. In fact, it snuck up on her. Nobody had asked her what she wanted, and she hadn't talked about it. It felt like bad luck. She knew it was probably crazy, but she thought she might only still be alive because of some sort of supernatural clerical error, and if she drew people's attention to the fact that she was still around, somebody would catch their mistake and zap her into the grave. Dumb, but there it was.

"Happy birthday," Dad said in the morning. "I'm glad you were born." He'd been saying this on her birthday for as long as she could remember, and it was corny, but also very sweet. "Do you want your present now or later?"

"Hmmm," Brianna said. "I guess later." It was probably an Old Navy gift card or some CDs that Dad got with his employee discount at Bargain Zone. Well, it would be fun to get something.

"Are you sure?" Dad asked.

"Yeah, I'm sure."

"I think you might actually enjoy your day a little more if you have this present."

"Okay," Brianna said. Well, that pretty much ruled out the Old Navy gift card. Still, maybe it was a CD that he thought she might like to listen to.

"Great!" Dad beamed. "Follow me." He started walking toward the garage, and the only thing Brianna could think was that her present was probably pretty small if he could fit it in between the weights and all the bikes in there.

"Now, there were some delays, and I'm really sorry it's not completely ready, but I wanted you to know it was coming." Dad threw open the garage door. "Happy birthday!"

Brianna peered around him and saw what was, or possibly would be, a motorcycle. It was a small one—looked like it had started life as a 150 cc Honda or something. It was still mostly in pieces, but the gas tank was painted to resemble a killer whale. When Brianna was younger, she'd been obsessed with marine mammals. She'd always liked the killer whales because they were fierce and mean, and the fact that they couldn't breathe in the place where they spent most of their lives didn't hold them back from being fearsome predators.

"Oh my God!" she yelled. "Dad! Is that really for me?"

"Yeah, sweetie, it is."

"How did you . . . When did you . . . It's so awesome! Oh my God, this is the best present I've ever seen!" She threw her arms around him. "Thank you thank you thank you!"

Dad looked thrilled. "You're welcome. I hope you like it. We have to teach you how to ride it and get you a license and everything, so I'm sorry, because it's not—"

"Dad, shut up! I love it!"

She got dressed and medicated as quickly as she could and then hopped into the Sunfire. She patted the dashboard and said, "It won't be long until you're second choice, pal."

Melissa and Stephanie both gave her cards and told her they were kidnapping her after school. "To go where?" she asked.

"It's a surprise."

"Okay."

In homeroom, Adam was clutching an MIT application. "Got your recommendations yet?" he asked.

"Adam, the application isn't due for months."

"Yeah, well, I guess I'm a little excited. I've already asked Ms. Kellie for one. You should totally ask Eccles. He loves you."

"Ew, don't be gross."

"I don't mean like that. I mean in a teacher's pet way, which isn't necessarily a bad thing. Anyway, he'll probably write a great recommendation."

Brianna didn't know if it was annoying or good that Adam was going to be making sure she got every step of the application done.

"Yeah, I guess you're right. I'll ask him today."

"Cool. Now, have you looked at the essays yet?"

"Adam, you seriously need to relax. If you have any more questions about what I've done yet, the answer is nothing."

Adam grinned. "Sorry. Geeking out a little bit. Just walking around campus and picturing myself there and thinking about getting out of this place—I just can't wait to get out of here."

It was more complicated for Brianna. She had been excited at MIT, but she wanted to make this year last because it could represent as much as five percent of her time on earth, and she wasn't going to wish it away. Before she could tell Adam any of this, or question whether this was a conversation she really wanted to get into before eight in the morning, the bell rang.

"Oh, by the way," Adam said as they were dismissed, "happy birthday." He handed her a card and practically ran out of homeroom. How had he known it was her birthday, anyway?

The front of the card had this muscular guy with a big sword killing a dragon. Inside, it said, "I wanted to make sure there'd be no draggin' around on your birthday!"

Adam had written, "I thought about getting a less geeky card, but I do have an image to maintain. Happy Birthday."

She stowed the card in her bag and went to class.

Even though she knew Adam was right, Brianna was nervous about asking Eccles for a recommendation.

She hung back after class, and Adam gave a discreet thumbs-up, and left her alone with the teacher.

"Um, Mr. Eccles?"

Eccles looked up from rooting through a desk drawer and grinned. "Ms. Pelletier! How can I help you?"

"Well, I've decided to get myself to a dormitory, and I was just wondering . . ." She trailed off. What was she supposed to say? Can you write something about how wonderful I am? She knew teachers did this stuff all the time, but it was still really hard to ask.

"You were wondering if I could write you a recommendation?"

Brianna blushed. "Yeah."

"Ms. Pelletier, it would be my pleasure. It is so rare that I get to write a recommendation for someone with such a brilliant mathematical mind. Your recommendation practically writes itself."

Now Brianna was really embarrassed. She managed to thank

him and added, "Obviously I'm not going to see it or anything, but I really want them to know I can do math, you know, not just that I'm sick."

"Ms. Pelletier, it would never even cross my mind to mention anything but your mathematical ability. Though I do hope your own essay will pull tears from the eyes of the hardest-hearted admissions counselor."

"Oh, I'm gonna milk it for all it's worth. It's caused me enough trouble, I figure the least it can do is get me into MIT."

Eccles laughed. "Fantastic. I shall begin your recommendation with all due dispatch."

"Thanks a lot. I appreciate it."

"Yes, time is short."

Brianna suddenly felt bad, like he thought she wanted to make sure he wrote it before he croaked. "Oh, jeez, I didn't mean . . ."

"Oh, I know, Ms. Pelletier. Forgive me. I'm sorry to drag mortality into the discussion. It's never far from my mind, but that's no reason I should trouble you."

"Don't worry about it. It's never far from my mind either."

It was strange to have this kind of moment with a teacher, but it was really nice, too. They completely understood each other. Brianna felt better about herself, because here was this guy who had all these years of pondering things that were impossible to understand, and when it came to looking at the end of his life, he was scared, too.

"I do think about what you said, though, with the math, and everything. It makes me feel better sometimes."

"I'm glad, Ms. Pelletier. One tiny good deed to weigh against a lifetime of . . . Well, in any case, I'm glad if something I've said has provided comfort. I've come to believe more and more that our mission is less to discover the beauty of the universe through mathematics and more to simply be kind to our fellow creatures."

Eccles suddenly looked incredibly old and sad, and Brianna felt sorry for him. She had a weird thought—maybe the only good thing about dying young was that she hadn't built up a lifetime of regrets. When she thought about her life, she remembered a couple of times in middle school when she'd been really mean, and some of the times when she took out her bad feelings on Dad because he was the closest target. But she hadn't done anything bad enough to feel like she'd made the world worse. All the years Eccles had been teaching, all the kids he'd helped get into college, all the kids who he'd shown that there were other, bigger things to think about besides who looked at you in the cafeteria, and he obviously still felt like his equation wasn't balanced.

Eccles shook his head. "My apologies once again for waxing philosophical. I shall have your recommendation complete by next week."

"Thanks so much. And don't worry about the philosophy. I can handle it."

Eccles smiled. "Your generosity of spirit is inspirational."

"Okay, well, I've gotta go prove Zeno wrong and eat a tuna salad sandwich."

"Do enjoy," Eccles said.

"I shall," Brianna said. And she did.

this perfect night

At the end of the day, Brianna met Melissa and Stephanie by Stephanie's locker.

She felt lighter even though her bag seemed to weigh as much as she did. It was her birthday, so she was going to celebrate and try not to think about life or death, and she'd get to laugh with her friends, and maybe that was the best thing you could do with your life anyway.

As they reached the foot of the staircase by the parking lot, Brianna saw Ashley running down the stairs.

"Bri!" Ashley called out.

"Hey, Ash, what's up?"

"Oh my God, I've been looking for you all day! Happy birthday!" she said, and she placed a card in Brianna's hand.

"Hey, thanks!" Brianna said.

"So, do you have any big plans?"

"Well"—she nodded at Stephanie and Melissa—"apparently, but I don't know what they are yet."

"Cool! Happy birthday," Ashley said as a couple of her identical little friends came and swept her away.

"Come on!" Stephanie said. "We're gonna be late. Make sure you bring your coat."

They all piled into Melissa's car because she was the most fearless driver. Brianna was not a fearless passenger, though, and she held on to the door as they sped through the back roads, convinced Melissa was going to crash.

But Melissa didn't crash, and when they pulled up to the docks, Brianna still didn't know what they were doing. "People are getting on already!" Stephanie cried. "Do you have the tickets?"

"Yes," Melissa replied calmly, and Brianna looked at the boat that was loading. It was a whale-watch boat. It was actually the same whale-watch boat that they had all taken on a field trip in the fifth grade.

"Oh my God, you guys, this is so sweet!" Brianna said.

"Less talking, more running," Melissa responded. "We're gonna miss it if we don't hurry, and this is the very last one before they shut down for the winter."

They ran up the gangway and found seats inside the boat. There were seats outside, but it would be way too freezing out there. Brianna remembered being on this same boat seven years ago, and how she and her best friend Melissa had made friends with a new girl named Stephanie.

The boat started chugging out to sea, and Brianna said, "You guys, this is a completely awesome birthday present." Melissa and Stephanie beamed. They spent an hour talking and laughing, and then the captain came over the PA and announced, "Folks, if you look off the starboard side—that's the right for those of you not used to ocean travel—you'll see something pretty spectacular."

He hadn't even finished speaking when a gigantic humpback came up, blew a gigantic breath, and disappeared with a splash of its gigantic tail. It had been years since Brianna's cetacean obsession had faded away, but all at once she felt it flooding back. This animal was—there was no other word for it—magnificent. She stared at the water where the humpback's tail had made a big splash.

Suddenly she heard giggling. She turned around. "What?" she said.

"It's just," Stephanie said, "don't get mad, but you're so cute . . . you looked at that whale like, I don't know—"

"Like Stephanie looks at the football team," Melissa said, and they all started laughing.

They saw a few right whales, which would have been really cool if they hadn't already seen a humpback, and then, as it grew dark, the boat headed back to Blackpool Harbor. Brianna felt herself lulled to sleep by the gentle motion of the boat and the hum of the engines, and when they docked, she awoke between a sleeping Melissa and a sleeping Stephanie.

They went and had dinner at Stephanie's and watched *American Pie* for probably the hundredth time, even though it was really just background noise while they talked.

Finally Brianna went home at midnight, exhausted. If only, she thought, there were some way to save this perfect night, so she could revisit it whenever she wanted, so she could feel the way she felt now and never have to feel sad or afraid or lonely again. She understood the idea of ending it all while things were good, so she wouldn't have to slip away in some hospital bed somewhere, but she wasn't ready to ramp off the Tobin Bridge just yet. Besides, while the idea of the jump was kind of cool, the reality would be terrifying. She didn't want to go out feeling like she was too scared to take the death she had coming to her.

And, anyway, maybe there'd be a breakthrough treatment, she'd live after all, and she'd go to MIT. Dr. Patel was always talking about this and that drug or therapy that was "in the pipeline," and maybe if she could hold on long enough, things would be okay.

broken

One week later, Brianna was wide awake at four o'clock on a Saturday morning. She lay in bed imagining a life for herself: a wonderful life where she was sitting next to the Charles River in her maroon sweatshirt with a graphing calculator, watching the sailboats in the sun and feeling her brain buzzing with satisfaction. Maybe she'd even have a boyfriend, a guy who would think she was interesting and cool. It could happen. It could all happen.

She looked at the clock: 4:27. Dad had to work today, so she'd be up in an hour anyway. She got out of bed and looked at the MIT application. The two short essays would be a breeze, writing about what she'd bring to the community and what was her biggest academic passion. Then, in the long essay section, was choice B, the one she'd been looking for: "Describe the biggest challenge you've faced in your life and explain how you overcame it."

Brianna took out a pen and a notebook and dashed off the "I'm a poor kid with CF, let me in" essay. English was never her strongest subject, but she thought she'd nailed her conclusion:

I don't get to say I've overcome cystic fibrosis. It's in my DNA, so it will always be with me. I'll be living with my challenge until I die. I spent a long time feeling bad about how unfair that is, but I found that being mad about something I can't change was just getting in the way of my enjoyment of whatever time I do have. I can't change my DNA, but I did change the way I feel about it, and, in some ways, that felt like an even bigger challenge.

She couldn't imagine anybody reading this and not letting her in.

She ate and got percussed and said goodbye to Dad and was still wide awake. It was only seven o'clock. Too early to call anybody, and she didn't feel like watching TV. Her mind was racing. She'd fed the MIT fantasy, and, as though her mind wanted to balance out the hope she dared to feel with some despair, she started to be afraid that she'd just had her last birthday.

Despite the chilly November breeze, she decided to go to the beach. Maybe if she contemplated the number of waves or grains of sand, she'd get some deep thoughts like Eccles did, and maybe she'd feel better.

When she got there, the sun had been up for only a few minutes, and she was disappointed to see that she didn't have the beach to herself. There was a blue folding chair that some fat guy was sitting in. Brianna realized it had to be Eccles. She hadn't even thought about the fact that he was supposed to be there early every morning.

She crept around to the front of the chair and saw that she was right. His eyes were closed, and Brianna suddenly knew Eccles had died on the beach. Well, she thought, that was probably the way he wanted to go out. No, he couldn't really be dead. She couldn't see him breathing, though. Should she call 911? Was it actually an emergency if somebody was dead?

"Mr. Eccles?" she said quietly. Nothing. Shit. She felt guilty because her first thought was "What about my recommendation?"

"Mr. Eccles!" she said louder. And this time, thankfully, he shook his head and slowly opened his eyes.

"Ms. Pelletier . . ." he said. When he spoke, she got a whiff of stale booze breath that almost knocked her out.

"Um, are you okay?" she asked.

He thought for a few seconds before answering. "In the near term, with the exception of the typical symptoms of excessive alcohol consumption, the answer seems to be yes. I'm not in any immediate danger. However"—he stretched and shifted in the chair—"my cardiologist informed me yesterday that my latest test reveals significant degradation in a number of key . . . Well, I suppose I shouldn't give you the gory details. Suffice it to say that I'm a bit closer to the limit of my particular function than I had assumed."

Brianna didn't know what to say. She knew what it was like to get bad news from doctors, but she'd never gotten news that bad. Not yet. "I'm sorry," she said, and as if on cue, she started to cough. Fortunately it stopped before it got too bad, and she was spared having to fight off the post-tussive emesis.

"Well," Eccles said, "I appreciate that. And your presence here has mitigated the shock of waking up on the beach."

"Thanks." Brianna smiled.

"So what brings you to the beach so early this morning?" Eccles asked, rubbing his eyes.

"I couldn't sleep. Contemplating the infinite and stuff like that. My birthday was last week—"

"Happy birthday! Welcome to legal adulthood."

"I actually hit legal adulthood a year ago. I missed a lot of school in elementary school. Anyway, I just started to wonder, what if it's my last birthday, you know?"

"All too well."

"And I guess I thought it might help to be here and think about waves or prime numbers or something."

"Well, I hope it works better for you than it did for me. I turned to the treacherous embrace of single malt scotch. You see, mathematics is not always enough to comfort me."

Brianna stood silently next to Eccles, and they watched the waves break. Here we are, Brianna thought, alone together. "Alone Again Or." And then, just for a few seconds, she thought of nothing. And when she realized that she'd been thinking nothing, she wondered if that was what it was like to be dead.

Whoa.

Suddenly Eccles started talking as though they were in the middle of a conversation. "I find that it's been very easy for me to talk about the unimaginable for decades, and what I've said to you about being both one and infinite, about joining the mysteries I've devoted my professional life to, well, I meant all of that. It's just that it's one thing to say such things when you believe you're only talking in the abstract. But now that I'm faced with the very real possibility of my death—a wiser man would have seen the cardiac incident of the summer as an indication that this was a real possibility, but I'm not that man— In any case, I'm simply terrified."

Brianna didn't know what to say. Shut up, you're freaking me out? You're the guy with the answers, and if you don't know anything, how can I possibly ever know anything? Go talk to somebody else about this, why are you talking to me?

Neither of them spoke. Finally, just to try to get the conversation onto a track that felt a little more comfortable, Brianna said, "I'm sorry. Do you have family around here or anything?"

Eccles didn't answer. He just stared out at the sea. The tide was going out.

The silence started to get awkward. Brianna shifted her weight from one side to another.

Finally, Eccles spoke. His voice sounded funny and quiet. "Well, that's a difficult question. You'll forgive me. If I weren't staring into the abyss and hungover to boot, I probably would make up some glib answer that avoids the reality, but right now my ability to bullshit seems to be compromised.

"You know at the end of *The Wizard of Oz*, when the wizard protests that he's not a bad man, just a very bad wizard?"

"Um, yeah."

"Well, the reverse is true for me. I know I am good at my job, but I still struggle with everything else. As long as my mind is in the beautiful realm of mathematics, I am in my element. But the real world is so much messier, so much more difficult to navigate.

"I'm beating around the bush telling you something it's probably inappropriate for me to tell you anyway, but since we stand at the edge of the same abyss . . . I was never a member of Love. I was a music student and played a few string parts on *Forever Changes*. I exploited the similarity between my name and that of the guitarist for years. I enjoyed the adulation that accompanied the rock star story. I suppose I was finally cool in high school. And not only high school, but throughout the community. I used to come to the beach in the summer, and people would flock to me to hear my tales of rock and roll excess.

"In any case, there was an indiscretion with someone who believed my exagger—— Ah, they were lies, weren't they? Yes. Well, my wife took my daughter, Grace, to California, and though I understand the ill will they both bear me, Grace won't return a phone call from her dying father."

Eccles's voice broke. Brianna looked over at him and saw that he had tears running down his cheeks.

"So there you have it. The man behind the curtain." He wiped the tears from his face. "I'm a pretty good wizard. I'm just not a very good man. And I can't stand looking at the end of a life that's been such a failure."

Brianna thought maybe she should be mad—she'd bought the lie about Love, and the fact that she thought she knew somebody in the band had definitely made her like the music more. But she wasn't mad. She actually felt sorry for Eccles. At school he was this jolly fat man, a popular teacher that everybody liked, but that wasn't who he was at all.

The one thing that was annoying right now was that his story had made her think of Mom, and that was something she hated thinking about even more than death.

Brianna counted seven waves breaking. She had to get out of there, but it was awkward. "I . . . um, have to go. I'm sorry, though. About everything. About your heart."

"Thank you, Ms. Pelletier. I'm afraid it's broken." Mr. Eccles put his head in his hands.

She left him alone with the sea and his regrets.

she should have stayed

Brianna drove around for hours, zooming up and down the streets, trying not to think about anything because almost everything hurt. The only thought she had that didn't hurt was that as much as it sucked to be her, it would suck even more to be Eccles.

Finally, when she'd been on every street in Blackpool, Brianna went home. Her phone rang almost as soon as she got inside. It was Ashley.

"Hi, Brianna," she said. "Do you want to . . . you know . . . get some ice cream or something?" Ashley sounded so tentative that it made Brianna sad. Had she made Ashley think she'd reject her? Had she been a bad friend, a bad mentor?

"Absolutely!" Brianna answered, with as much enthusiasm as she could.

"Cool!" Ashley said.

"Is everything okay with your folks?"

"Well, I can't really talk about it now, but no."

"I'm sorry," Brianna said. "Are they getting a divorce or something?"

"Yeah."

"Oh, that sucks."

"Yeah. Listen, I was talking about it all night with Mom, so I don't want to talk about it anymore. I'm sorry, I don't want to be mean . . ."

"Ash, you're not. I understand. There's all kinds of stuff I don't want to talk about or think about. So we'll just go and eat some ice cream, right?"

"Yeah."

"Great. If Melissa's working, we can probably even get it for free. I'll meet you there at three?"

"Perfect."

"Okay. And, Ashley?"

"Yeah?"

"I'm not gonna ask you about it or bug you about it, and if you never want to talk about it, that's totally cool, but you do know you *can* talk to me about it if you want, okay?"

"Yeah."

"Anytime at all. Middle of the night, whatever."

Ashley said quietly, "Thanks, Bri."

"That's what I'm here for."

She hung up and called Dad's phone.

"Hey, sweetie, what's up?" he said.

"Nothing," Brianna said, realizing only after she said it that she sounded tired. Eccles's story was weighing her down, Ashley's sadness was weighing her down, and she couldn't stop thinking about Mom, and that was *really* weighing her down.

"You okay, sweetie?"

"Yeah, Dad, I'm fine. Just tired, I guess."

"Okay. What are you doing with your day?"

"I dunno. I rode around this morning. I guess I'll work on my MIT application for a while or something. I'm meeting Ashley for ice cream later, so if I'm not here when you get home, that's where I am."

"Thank you. You sure you're okay?"

"I'm fine, Dad, really. I'll see you later."

"Okay," Dad said, his tone of voice saying "You're not fooling me with that 'I'm fine' lie, young lady."

She did spend most of the rest of the day working on her application, except for meeting Ashley at Hot Licks. They were both depressed, but it was nice to be depressed with somebody else for a little while.

When Dad finally got home, he came right to her room.

"Bri," he said, "we need to talk."

"Okay."

"Well, I've been thinking ever since we spoke this morning. I realized that I may have been kind of selfish."

"Dad, what are you talking about?" Brianna could certainly say Dad was annoying (and she frequently did), but she never would have called him selfish. Mom was a different story. But not Dad.

"I know you didn't want to apply to MIT, and watching you mope around while you're doing the application, I realized that you might be doing it to make me happy."

"Dad, I'm not—"

"Just let me finish, sweetie. I think I pushed you too hard, and I know you made me a promise to follow through on the application, but I want to let you know that I'm letting you out of your promise. You have to make yourself happy in this life, honey, and I don't want you worrying about making me happy. You do what you want to do, okay? I could never be any prouder of you than I am right now, and the only thing that will make me happy is you being happy."

Against her will, Brianna felt her eyes filling up with tears. Before she knew what was happening, she was hugging Dad and crying, and everything she'd been feeling—all the fear and sadness and dread and hope and love and everything—felt like too much, and so it all came pouring out.

"Dad, it's not the application. I actually want to do that."

Dad looked relieved. "Well, that's good. I was feeling so bad, you know, like I was making you miserable."

Brianna started laughing. "I guess I can be miserable without any help." Dad smiled, and then Brianna asked, "Why do you think Mom left?"

Of course they had talked about this before, but not for a long time. Mom's departure was a fact of their lives, and Dad had explained it to Brianna when it happened: "Mommy has to go away," he'd said, his voice breaking, "but she's still going to write and call and even though she's not here, she loves you very, very much." There didn't seem to be much to add to that, though Mom did send a letter saying she was sorry she had to go, and she kept sending letters after that, but when Brianna was ten, she started throwing them away without reading them. When she was eleven, she told Mom on the phone that she hated her and never wanted to talk to her again. And that had been that.

"I think you know, don't you?" Dad said. She knew, she knew that she was too sick and awful for Mom to love. "I mean, she's a very, very weak person, Bri. She's one of the weakest people I ever met. And she . . . she couldn't stand seeing you sick because she loved you too much."

"What do you mean?"

"I mean when you're a parent, you love your kid so much that seeing them sick or suffering is the worst thing in the world. Next time you're at Children's, look at the parents there. They're in hell because they can't protect the people they love more than anything. Anybody there would do anything, including die, to save their kids, but there's nothing they can do except wait and hope."

Dad put his hand on his forehead and closed his eyes. Brianna could hear him breathing. After a minute, he looked at her. His eyes were red. "And Mom loves you that much, even if she's horrible at showing it. She loves you that much, but she's not strong enough to watch you suffer. She's not strong enough to even think she might lose you. So she decided to take matters into her own hands. She inflicted this terrible wound on you because she's too much of a coward to face being wounded herself.

"But you should know, and I know this doesn't make any sense, but you being sick wouldn't have been so scary to her if she didn't love you so much."

"If she really loved me," Brianna said, "she should have stayed."

"Yeah," Dad finally said in a quiet voice, "she should've."

After what seemed like five minutes, Dad looked up. "I have her number and her address, you know. You can call her or write her if you want to."

"You still talk to her?"

"She calls about once a month to ask about you."

"And you actually talk to her?"

"Yeah."

"Why?"

"Because I want her to know what she's missing. And I want that to hurt." Neither one of them said anything for a minute. "Anyway, you can call her or write her if you want."

"Nah," Brianna said. "She doesn't deserve me."

Dad smiled. "No, sweetie, she doesn't. And you don't owe her anything. But she owes a lot to you."

"Yeah, but it's too late for that."

"Okay. Your decision, and I support you either way."

your little study date

Brianna woke up the next day feeling especially tired. Somewhere in the back of her mind, she wondered if this was something she should be worrying about, but she told herself that she was stressed out about everything she had to do.

Sunday was supposed to be the day of rest, but there was a big paper in English, a big paper in history, a big test in calc, and, oh yeah, her MIT application. She really wanted to polish it off today, but she knew if she sat around here all day, it would be impossible for her to do it. Every time she wanted to sit down and do it, she found herself doing other stuff. She knew it was because of her stupid irrational fear that completing the application would cause her to be struck dead for having the hubris (a good word she'd learned when they read *Oedipus* which was otherwise really boring) to hope for a future.

Well, there was nothing for it. If she was going to get this done, she needed Adam to make her do it.

As soon as it seemed like a decent hour, Brianna called Adam's house.

"Hey," he said. "You are so lucky. Jessica just left five minutes ago. Early flight. If she'd been here when you called . . . hoo boy. Trouble."

"Can you hear my eyes rolling?"

"Actually, I can. Did I go to the well one too many times on that joke?"

"At least. Listen, can I ask you a favor?"

"You can ask."

Brianna rolled her eyes again. God, the kid was a cornball. "Okay, well, I'm having a hard time making myself do the application, so I was hoping we could get together and you could bug me until I do it."

"Sure! I have a pantsload of work to do today, so I'd love some company."

"Great!" She hadn't thought this out very well. Her house was tiny and not that clean, and she didn't really like having anybody but Melissa and Stephanie and maybe Ashley over here. "So, do you wanna meet at Melville's or something? Maybe get some coffee?"

"Why don't you come over to my house? My mom made pie last night. I like to sit in the sunroom and look at the sea a little bit, and it makes homework a little more tolerable."

Wow. She knew from driving him home from MIT that Adam lived in East Blackpool, but she'd only seen the front of the house. If he had a sunroom with an ocean view, he must be even more loaded than she'd thought.

"Okay. When's a good time for you?"

"Well, how about one o'clock?"

"Great." Brianna hung up.

At one, she arrived at Adam's house. It was about five times the size of her house. Adam's mom showed her into the sunroom, which was like a big porch with windows on every wall. In the distance, the waves crashed against the shore, never stopping, each wave an integer, each wave an atom, each wave a point, each one an infinitesimal fraction of all the waves that ever were or ever would be.

"Hey!" Adam said as she walked into the sunroom. "You want some pie?"

"Um, sure," Brianna said.

"Oh, look, and here's Mom with two big slices now!"

Adam's mom, a tall, incredibly pale, kind of nerdy-looking woman (big surprise), said, "Just so you know, Brianna, I don't always wait on him. I'm trying to teach him a little bit about hospitality here, though it's probably a lost cause. Smart boy, but kind of clueless socially," she teased.

"Hey!" Adam said, grinning, "I resemble that remark!"

"See what I mean?" his mom said. "Gets that corny sense of humor from his father. I can't seem to break either of them of it."

She set the pie down, and Brianna thanked her. "You see, Adam?" Mrs. Pennington said. "That's what you do when someone does something nice for you!"

"Thanks, Mom. Can you get back in your cage now?"

This earned Adam a quick smack on the back of the head. "Only language he understands," Mrs. Pennington said, smiling.

"I'll remember that," Brianna promised.

"Hey, you only get to smack me if you make me pie first," Adam said.

"In your dreams," Brianna retorted. She popped a pill and took a forkful of the apple pie—it had those crisscrossed parts on the top and tasted amazing.

"So, what have you got done so far?" Adam asked.

"I've done a first draft of my essay," she said. "I asked everybody for recommendations. Now I just have all this other crap to fill out." Brianna indicated the forms with the basic personal information blanks.

"All right. Let's get to it. You wanna copy mine?"

"We have the same social security number all of a sudden?"

"I was joking, jeez."

Brianna realized another reason she hadn't done the forms. Because filling out all these forms was just like filling out medical forms. Here is my name and social security number. Here are the medications I am currently taking. Here is where I sign to indicate my understanding that there is a small but nonzero chance of my dying as a result of this procedure.

Still, with Adam looking on, she made herself do it. For about thirty seconds, until her phone rang. Melissa.

"Hey, Mel, what's up?"

"Freaking out. Totally freaking out. I have a test tomorrow, and I'm sorry, I know you already explained this stuff to me, but I really need help. I am totally going to fail."

"Okay, calm down. Do you want me to come over at four?"

"I can't, I have to work. Can you come over now?"

"No, I'm kind of . . . I'm in the middle of something."

She could hear Melissa's panic get overwhelmed by curiosity. "What are you in the middle of? Is Todd over there?"

"Ugh, God, no. I'm just over at Adam's getting some help with my MIT application."

"Tell her to come over," Adam said. "There's plenty of pie."

"Um, you wanna come over here?"

"I don't want to butt in on your little study date," Melissa said. "God, that is so cute! And I love the fact that you can't even deny it because he's sitting right there!"

"Yeah," Brianna said in a flat voice. "Here's Adam to tell you how to get here." She handed the phone to Adam and went back to filling out forms.

Melissa arrived fifteen minutes later, shown in to the sunroom by a beaming Mr. Pennington.

"Hi, Adam, thanks for letting me come over," Melissa said, smiling sweetly.

"No problem at all! You want some pie?"

Melissa looked at Brianna. "It's really good pie," Brianna said. "You should have some."

"Okay. So, Bri, I'm sorry, but can you look at this?" Melissa said, pulling a notebook out of her bag.

"I'm about halfway through this short answer question. Give me about five minutes."

"Maybe I can help?" Adam offered.

"Awesome," she said. "Thank you."

An hour and a half later, Brianna was done with her application and Melissa was no longer convinced she was going to fail her test and ruin her life.

They left together, and Melissa said, "He's really nice."

"Yes, he is," Brianna said.

"Don't worry, though, Bri, you can have him."

Brianna punched Melissa in the arm. "Would you shut up?"

Melissa laughed, and Brianna drove home feeling happy.

When Dad got home from work, she came out of her room, sealed envelope in hand, and popped it in his lap.

"Done!" she said.

"Hey, congratulations!" Dad said. "You want me to mail it for you?"

"Yeah, that would be great. I don't even want to look at that thing anymore."

"So, how are we gonna celebrate?" Dad asked.

Brianna suddenly found herself annoyed. "We can't celebrate unless I get in," she said. And she didn't say, Maybe not even then, because even if I get in, there's no guarantee I'll live long enough to go.

Dad must have seen the shadow cross her face. "What's the matter, honey?" he said. "You know, I called about some motorcycle lessons, and I think your bike will be ready by—"

"It's not that, Daddy. I just . . . I want to go, but, I'm just afraid . . ." Weird. She thought it all the time, but she couldn't make her mouth say the words.

"I know," Dad said. He got off the couch and hugged her and didn't say anything. There was nothing to say.

that's not living

Brianna woke up earlier than usual. She was grumpy and tired and kept snapping at Dad that he was doing the percussion all wrong.

"Hey," Dad stammered, "it sounds like . . . Your breathing . . . Do you think we should call Dr. Patel and maybe get you another nebulizer treatment?"

Brianna was furious. "No more nebs! They taste like hell and they don't work! No, no, no! I'm fine!"

Dad pounded on her in silence for a minute. "Honey, what's wrong?"

"Nothing is *wrong*, okay? I'm just grumpy."

"Okay." Pound, pound, pound. "Now, I'm not going to give you advice because I know you hate that."

"Good," Brianna said before coughing and spitting up a gob of phlegm.

"Nice one!" Dad said, and Brianna couldn't help smiling.

"Yeah, I try."

"Anyway, just listen to everything I have to say before you get mad, okay?"

Brianna knew that meant he was about to infuriate her, but once Dad got it into his head that he had something to say, there was no getting him to stop. "Okay."

"I want to tell you something about my life. Your mom took off because she was afraid of losing you."

"Dad, this isn't what I want to talk about first thing in the—"

"Wait. Let me finish. Now, I think that she made a terrible choice. I mean, I'm just as afraid as she is, but if I'd let that fear rule my life, I would have missed out on so much—pretty much everything that made my life worth living. I am not going to pull away from you because I'm afraid of losing you. I mean, a lot of people tell me not to ride my bike at all, even for the three miles from here to Bargain Zone because it's too dangerous, what if something bad happens? Well, I mean, what if it doesn't? Then at least I get a little fun in my day before I have to go make sure there are enough Dora the Explorer backpacks on the racks and fire a few of your classmates for getting high out back."

Brianna laughed. That happened about once a year, and it was never surprising and always amusing.

"So, that's it. The fact that things are scary doesn't mean you shouldn't do them. That's not living."

Brianna knew it was good advice, but she also knew that Dad was full of shit. If he was so bold about diving into life no matter what happened, why hadn't he dated anybody since Mom left? He was all about not being afraid of things he didn't really think were going to happen—he didn't really believe he'd wipe out on his bike. But he knew he could get his heart shredded because it had already happened, so he wouldn't give it to anyone else. Or else he was still carrying a torch for Mom. She didn't know which one was sadder.

"Hey," Dad said as he finished up the percussion, "you in there?"

"Yeah," Brianna said. "Thanks, Daddy."

"That's what I'm here for."

∞

Brianna got to school early and headed up to Eccles's room. He wasn't there, so she went to the caf for a few minutes. Melissa wasn't there, but Stephanie was. Brianna sat down and helped herself to Munchkins, and Stephanie started talking about how she was now ready to dump Tom who'd beaten up Kevin at the party because, she said, "He just isn't that nice to me."

Brianna resisted pointing out that if you decide to go out with a guy because you've seen him beating somebody up, it really shouldn't be such a shocker if he turns out not to be that nice. Stephanie went on and on about her bad luck, and Brianna finally said, "Maybe it's not your luck. Maybe it's the choices you're making. I mean, there are tons of nice guys out there, but they're probably not the ones getting into fights at parties." Oops. She'd said it anyway.

There was an uncomfortable silence and Brianna was really afraid that Stephanie was going to start crying or something.

Instead Stephanie just sighed and said, "Yeah. Maybe you're right. Let me know if you find any."

"You never have any trouble finding guys—you just have to pick the nice ones," Brianna said.

"I know," Stephanie agreed. "But there's something about dumb and good-looking that I can't resist."

"But, sweetie, it's making you miserable."

"Maybe I should just take a break from all guys for a while until I can figure out how to start liking better ones."

"Sounds like a plan," Brianna said. The bell rang and they both headed off to homeroom.

She felt winded by the time she got there. It was a trip she had made without getting winded countless times. Well, she was stressed out. She plopped down next to Adam.

He looked up with a big grin on his face. "Thank you so much!" he said.

"You're welcome? What are you thanking me for?"

"Duh! Two girls in my house! You should have seen the look my dad gave me. I honestly don't think he's ever been as proud of me as he was last night."

"That's great, I guess."

"So, this is hilarious. First he gives me this lecture about how it's important to play the field—like I've ever even been on the field! But, he says, I have to be careful about hurting people, and I shouldn't string two girls along at once."

Brianna knew it wasn't really nice to laugh, but she just couldn't help it.

Fortunately, Adam didn't seem to mind. "Wait," he said, laughing himself, "it gets better. This morning I found a *box of condoms* on my nightstand. Like he thinks I'm some kind of super stud or something."

"Eww! Eww!"

"I know. My dad's delusional. But still, it was a pretty big deal to him. And to me, too. It was nice to be included."

She had an urge to tell him that there weren't that many nice people out there, that being nice was more important than being popular, that she could see his future stretching out, and it looked a lot better than Jim's or Kendrick's or any of those guys who never got picked on, who enforced the code of conformity in the halls by making fun of chubby goth girls and teasing sick kids about joining the football team.

But it would have been weird to say that, so she just smiled and said, "Well, it was nearly painless for us, too."

"Hmm. Next time I'll be sure to sing. Then it'll be *really* painful."

a marvel

After calc class ended, Brianna approached Eccles's desk, and she saw him digging out a Tupperware full of salad.

He looked up and got kind of red-faced. "Ms. Pelletier. I must apologize for . . ."

"No, you mustn't. I'm pretty sure teachers get to be human beings once a year or so."

Eccles smiled, but he was obviously off-balance and embarrassed, and he didn't seem to know what to say. She decided to bail him out.

"No Fluffernutter today?" she asked.

"No, sadly, I am on a rather Spartan diet that no longer includes that fantastic confection. It appears that I prefer a low-fat, intoxicant-free life in which I subsist on steamed vegetables and brown rice to dancing with the primes, at least for the moment. I may buy myself some time this way, and if that time is perhaps less rich than it otherwise might have been, I find I prefer having the time to not having the time. So you can add cowardice to the list of my flaws, because what I believed to be a rock-solid conviction melted away like so much—"

"Marshmallow Fluff?"

Eccles actually gave a laugh. "Yes, like that."

"Well, enjoy your lunch."

Eccles brandished the Tupperware. "Sadly, food and enjoyment are now divorced in my life."

"Sorry about that," Brianna said. "Hey, listen, can I ask you something?"

"Certainly."

"Since you're a good wizard and everything . . . I've been so focused on getting my application done—thank you for the recommendation, by the way—"

"My pleasure."

"Anyway, now that it's done, I've got nothing else to focus on till graduation. And so I'm pondering infinity again and wondering what might make my infinitesimal significant. You know? Like what if I don't make it to MIT? How will I know that my infinitesimal collection of atoms was significant at all?" Brianna blushed. It definitely still felt weird that she would say something like this to a teacher. She guessed with Molly gone, Eccles was her new illness mentor, whether he liked it or not.

"I'm not sure I have a good answer for that one," Eccles said. "I suppose I'm supposed to look back on my years of teaching and all the students who've gotten excited about math, who've gotten into MIT, who've done interesting things because I encouraged them, and feel like my life was worthwhile, but somehow that falls short."

Imagine how I feel, Brianna thought. You've at least had decades of teaching. People will remember you. I've got nothing.

"But I do have an encouraging thought," he said.

"What's that?"

"Do you know why I love mathematics?"

"Because it blew your mind for free when you couldn't get drugs?"

Eccles snorted in surprise. "Well, yes, but there's another reason. At the beginning of the course, I spoke of the power of math, and how it allows us to lift planes off the ground and so forth. Do you remember?"

Brianna nodded.

"I only say that stuff to try to hook in the kids who need for everything to have a practical application to feel like it's worthwhile. But here is why I really love mathematics: it's beautiful. When you can solve a complex equation, when you see the amazing concepts that people have come up with to solve problems, to explain things, to create a system that hangs together . . . Well, to me, it's just incredibly beautiful. It's like a cathedral is, I suppose, to some people. It's a marvel."

"Okay . . ." Brianna said, not sure exactly how this related to her question.

"So, you see, it's not what it can do that makes math beautiful. Its existence isn't justified by the 747s or any of the big mechanical things that it makes possible. Its existence is something to be celebrated because it is a beautiful, wonderful, incredibly complicated marvel."

"Yeah?"

"Yes. And so, Ms. Pelletier, are you."

Brianna blushed. "Thanks" was all she could get out.

"Anytime, Ms. Pelletier," Eccles said. Smiling, he opened his Tupperware and started eating his salad.

∞

After dinner, Dad asked her for help with the computer.

"Sure," Brianna said. She followed Dad to the computer. Next to it was his notebook and a battered manila folder bulging with receipts. "Oh, you haven't been using the spreadsheets at all, have you?"

"Well, I've just been so busy putting the bikes together . . ."

Brianna looked at the notebook and the stack of receipts. The man was hopeless. "Okay, Dad, I'll show you how to do this again. But I'm gonna need a big dish of ice cream."

"Coming right up," Dad promised.

A half hour later, they were caught up to two weeks before. Then Melissa called. "Hi," Brianna said, holding the phone with her shoulder and entering receipt amounts into the spreadsheet.

"Do you have a minute? I think I finally understand my math homework, but I really want to double-check."

Brianna looked at the stack of receipts. She knew she'd be forever on the phone, and Dad would be hovering, and then she'd never want to get back to this heinous task.

"Yeah, but can I call you in an hour? Or . . . Do you want Adam's number?"

There was a pause as Melissa considered that. "Okay, cool."

Brianna gave her the number and promised, "I'll call you later."

"You'd better," Melissa said, and Brianna could hear the smile in her voice.

An hour and a half later, Brianna was confident that Dad could do this himself if he ever bothered to try it, and she was about to call Melissa back when Ashley called her. Her parents were fighting again, and Brianna spent twenty minutes talking her through it.

Then she called Melissa, and they talked until Brianna was too tired to continue. She crawled into bed exhausted but happy.

better than this

The following week, Brianna found Ashley by her locker. "Mel and Steph and I are going to a party on Friday night. Do you want to come along and spend the night at my house?" she asked.

Ashley looked thrilled. "Oh, definitely. There's no place in the house where I can not hear the fighting, and I think I'm damaging my hearing turning my iPod up so loud."

On Wednesday at lunch, Melissa called out to Adam as he walked by, brown paper bag in hand. "Do you want to join us?"

Adam was definitely improving. He managed to wipe the "Oh yeah, right, you're messing with me" look off his face almost immediately and came walking over to their table like it was something he always did.

"Well, you know the cheerleading squad is expecting me over on the other side of the caf, but I guess I can stand to make 'em a little jealous," he said.

Melissa just looked at him. "Stephanie and I are *on* the cheerleading squad, moron."

Adam paused, but only for a second. "Hmm. Well, in that case, I have to go over there and make *you* jealous."

Everybody laughed. And by the end of lunch, Melissa had invited Adam to come to the party on Friday night, and a bunch of jocks had walked by their table with their mouths hanging open, like they couldn't believe Adam was really sitting there.

∞

Friday arrived, and Brianna asked Ashley if her mom could drop her off at six o'clock.

"You remember Ashley's coming over tonight, right?" she asked Dad when he got home from work.

"Yeah. Is she going to need me to do percussion in the morning?"

"Nah, she has a vest." Brianna said this casually, hoping she'd managed to keep the envy out of her voice, since she didn't want Dad to get depressed about how he couldn't provide her with the latest CF technology. Still, Brianna lusted after this stuff the way most kids lusted after new cell phones and iPods, and she wasn't sure she'd managed to stay cool.

If she had revealed her envy of Ashley's CF toys, Dad didn't seem to have noticed. "Okay, sweetie. And you guys are going to whose house?"

"I can't remember, some kid Stephanie knows. Oh, and I don't know if Cindy's on board with this, so if you could maybe keep that part of tonight's activities secret, that would be a big help."

"Bri, I'm not gonna lie to her."

This was bad for the party plan. "Well, okay, but that doesn't mean you have to actually volunteer anything, right?"

Dad laughed and said, "You sure you don't want to go to law school?" Brianna smiled, knowing that wasn't a question Dad really expected her to answer. "All right, all right. I won't volunteer anything."

Dad headed back to his room to change out of his Bargain Zone outfit. And while he was there, Brianna realized he hadn't given her his customary pre-party warnings about booze and sex. Those were always annoying, but it felt strange not to hear them. When he got back, dressed in his filthy coveralls—it was too cold to work in the garage in a sleeveless T-shirt anymore—she said, "Hey, you don't need to worry about booze and sex and stuff, by the way."

"Yeah, Bri, I know." Dad said this like she was the annoying one telling him obvious things. What was that about?

"How do you know? I could be planning to get hammered and sleep with the first guy I see!"

Dad just rolled his eyes. "I know you're not going to do anything with Ashley there except look out for her." Brianna was stunned. Dad continued, "Okay, then, I'm going to go out and work on this bike. Orders are starting to stack up."

∞

After dinner, Ashley and Brianna drove the Sunfire to a strip mall parking lot in East Blackpool to pick up Melissa, Stephanie, and Adam.

"So where exactly is this place?" Brianna asked Stephanie.

"Front Street somewhere," Stephanie said. "We'll know it when we see it."

"Front Street?" Brianna said. "Do they let West Blackpool trash into their parties over there?" She glanced at Ashley and saw her looking uncomfortable and immediately felt guilty. The whole East/West Blackpool thing was such a part of her conversations with Melissa and Stephanie that she hadn't even thought about the fact that Ashley lived in East Blackpool.

Fortunately, Melissa bailed her out. "Yeah, this party's only for West Blackpool trash. So, Ashley, you're going to need to look a little sluttier. You can copy Steph's look if you want." Stephanie punched Melissa's arm, but Melissa pretended not to notice.

Ashley laughed and said, "I, um, I thought I *had* dressed slutty."

"Oh, kid, you have lots to learn. You can't hang out with Brianna if you want to be trashy. Now my friend Steph here . . ." Melissa said, ducking the punch that came her way.

"Your friend Steph is about to give you an old-fashioned West Blackpool beatdown," Stephanie said, "like my old man taught me before he got locked up."

Melissa laughed and gave Stephanie a shove. "Bring it!"

Just then, Adam came running across the parking lot. "Whoa, whoa, whoa, ladies," he said, stepping between them and holding out his palms. "I can't *believe* you were gonna have a girlfight before I got here. I mean, I thought we were friends, Melissa."

"Ew, we were before you started being pervy," Melissa replied.

"Before I started being pervy? But you didn't know me when I was eleven," Adam protested.

Brianna had to jump in. "Adam, will you shut up and get in the car? And do you know Ashley?"

Adam turned, saw Ashley for the first time, and turned almost purple with embarrassment. "Oh, hi! I, um, I hope you know I'm just joking. I'm not usually, I mean, when I'm with friends I tend to . . ."

Ashley said, "Nice to meet you," and stuck out her hand, which worked as well as anything would have to get Adam to shut up.

They drove up and down Front Street three times before Stephanie felt like she knew where the party was. Both Adam and Ashley, going to their first BHS party, must have been nervous, but Brianna noticed they dealt with it in very different ways. She preferred Ashley's way—she just looked wide-eyed and terrified. Adam, on the other hand, was motor-mouthing from the backseat, chattering nonstop about basically nothing.

"So I have to wonder if the guys who torment me in the locker room are going to be there. The boys' locker room is really a *Lord of the Flies* experience. I mean, I have no idea what the girls' locker room is like. Of course I saw *Carrie* and *Porky's*, but I have to doubt that those are really accurate representations. I mean, it's not like they're blowing on the conch shell and chanting 'Kill the pig' in the boys' locker room, but they might as well be. All the veneer of civilization seems to disappear as soon as the Abercrombie & Fitch T-shirts are off, and—"

"Jesus, will you shut up?" Brianna said as she parked the Sunfire behind a line of much newer, much nicer cars. Apparently Melissa had lied about this party being just for West Blackpool trash.

Of course, despite the fact that it was a much bigger house than the ones they were usually in, it was just a BHS party. Kegs and shots out back, music too loud, and people milling around. Once they were inside, Melissa and Stephanie went off to mingle, while Adam and Ashley clung to Brianna like remoras on a shark.

They essentially stuck to the pattern they had begun in the car, and Brianna thought she might actually have to kill Adam, who would not stop yammering.

"This is kind of interesting from a sociological perspective. My only experience with the larger BHS society is in the cafeteria, and I certainly see borders being crossed here that aren't crossed at school. Is that just the presence of the alcohol, or would those two over there normally be hanging out outside of school?"

"Adam, will you please go get a drink?" Brianna hesitated to recommend booze, but if Adam had a drink, he would at least be unable to talk while he had a mouth full of liquid, and a plastic cup full of Milwaukee's Best might actually mellow him out a little.

"Yeah, okay, sure," Adam said. "Something for the ladies?"

Ashley looked at Brianna for her cue.

"I'm all set," Brianna said.

"Yeah, me too," Ashley agreed.

Adam waded through the crowd of partygoers just as Melissa came up with their friends Brian and Cathy. "Who invited Pennington?" Brian asked. "Is this like a chess club meeting or something?"

Cathy laughed, and Brianna was getting ready to say something when Melissa beat her to it. "Aren't we getting a little old for that cliquey stuff? Jocks and nerds; it's so ninth grade. No offense, Ashley, you're obviously more mature than most seniors. I mean, we're adults now. Do we have to keep acting like we're picking kickball teams on the playground?"

Brian looked puzzled, and Cathy said, "We're gonna go get some drinks."

They melted into the crowd, and Melissa said, "Am I wrong? The whole thing just seems so childish."

"Mel, don't you think we would have said the same thing two months ago if we'd seen him at a party?"

"Yeah, we probably would have. But, I mean, I just think it's time to grow up. God, I'm sick of this party already. Do you guys wanna go get a movie or something?"

Ashley looked disappointed, and Brianna felt guilty. Maybe this whole thing had been a terrible idea. Just then, Adam returned, looking considerably less steady than the last time they'd seen him. He had a plastic cup full of beer in his hand.

"You know, I think the whole thing was a setup to embarrass her or me, but it turns out I just did a body shot off Jenny Santangelo."

Brianna, Melissa, and Ashley looked at Adam, slack-jawed. He kept talking. "Sure, her friends were all laughing, but I figure the joke's on them. After all, I *licked* Jenny Santangelo! Her clavicle is—"

"All right, Adam, enough," Brianna said. "How much exactly have you had to drink in the last five minutes?"

"One shot of tequila, accompanied by salt, which I—"

"Licked off Jenny Santangelo. We know, we know."

Just then, Kevin, Stephanie's ex who had been replaced by Tom, staggered up to them. "Hey," he said to Melissa, "where's the whore?"

Melissa would surely have come up with a fantastic reply, but, unfortunately for everybody, Adam beat her to it.

"Aw, jeez, we left your mom on the corner!" he said. "Were we supposed to pick her up?"

Brianna would have thought that three and a half years on the bottom rung of the high school social ladder would have taught Adam not to mouth off to drunken football players, but apparently it hadn't, or else the tequila had overcome whatever common sense he possessed. Kevin flattened Adam with one punch to the face. He lay on the floor, stunned, with blood pouring out of his nose, and Kevin spat on him. "Pretty funny, faggot," Kevin said, and staggered away.

Melissa was right. This was a disaster. And Melissa was right about something else, too—trying to introduce Adam into this stupidity was dumb not because he wouldn't fit in but because he was actually better than this. They all were.

They helped Adam to his feet and pretended not to see the snot that was mixing with the blood running from his nose as he wiped himself off with tissues from Brianna and Ashley.

Melissa, after making sure Adam was okay, went off to find Stephanie and promised to get a ride and meet them back at her house. As they were walking out the door, Adam seemed to recover his sense of humor.

"Well, if this was a movie, the whole school would be chanting my name right now or some hot girl would thank me for standing up to him."

Brianna felt too awful to say anything. It was nice of him to stand up for Stephanie, even though she wasn't there to appreciate it. She was probably off making out with some other troglodyte even while they took her bloodied defender home.

"If this was a movie," Ashley said, "I don't think there would be this much blood."

They didn't say anything else until they got into the car. "That guy's hated me since I refused to eat his jockstrap in the ninth grade," Adam said.

They went back to Melissa's. Her mom was up and fussed over Adam, putting ice on his nose and cleaning him up and telling him what a wonderful young man he was to stand up for his friend.

Melissa got home with Stephanie, who immediately ran to Adam's side. "She was breaking up with Tom out back," Melissa whispered.

After thanking Adam profusely, Stephanie drew Brianna aside. "Why did he do that? Was he drunk or something?"

"No, Steph. Well, yes, he was, but that's not why he did it. He did it because he's your friend and he doesn't want idiots calling you names."

Stephanie looked over at Adam, who had wads of tissue up his nostrils. "That was nice. Dumb, but nice."

"Yeah."

Mrs. D'Amico made popcorn, and they went down to Melissa's basement and watched *Not Another Teen Movie* and had a much better time than they'd had at the party.

Finally Brianna took Adam to his house ("My Dad winked at me and told me he wouldn't wait up," Adam said, looking at his watch. "I'm afraid I'm going to disappoint him coming home at midnight") and drove home with Ashley.

After they checked in with Dad, they lay in the dark for a long time, talking. Ashley had a crush on some kid who was in the play with her, a sophomore. She was doing really well on her treatments and had gotten pats on the head from Dr. Patel the last time she went in.

Brianna was due to see Dr. Patel, and she could tell that whatever she told Dad, it was just about time for another ineffective nebulizer treatment. Things were getting worse, and she was heading for another hospitalization. She wanted to tell Ashley this, but she was supposed to help the kid, not bum her out.

Eventually Ashley fell asleep, but Brianna lay awake with her unspoken worries echoing in her head.

Molly, Molly, she thought, why can't you help me? Where are you?

Nobody answered, and eventually Brianna fell asleep.

a pretty nice thing to do

Another month passed. Brianna, Stephanie, Adam, and Melissa started hiding from the December cold at Melville's after school, drinking coffee and doing their homework. Brianna liked it because it felt way more collegiate than going to somebody's house and having their mom bring them pie while they studied. Even though Adam's mom did make killer pie and Adam's motor-mouthed tendencies were worse when he was under the influence of cappuccino.

When she hassled him to do it, Dad was actually able to keep his own books for his side business. Everything was fine. Except.

Brianna could feel herself getting sicker. After all these years, she knew exactly what was happening. It was getting a lot harder to breathe and her digestion was getting worse. She knew it wouldn't be long until she spiked a fever and she'd have to go back to the hospital to get flushed out and go on IV antibiotics to kill whatever was growing in the gunk in her lungs and guts.

She didn't tell Dad and she didn't call the doctor. She tried to ignore the evidence her body was throwing at her every day. Because she didn't want to be poor, sick little Brianna. She wanted to be strong, competent, genius-going-to-MIT Brianna, the one who was more or less normal. Not the one who spent days or maybe even weeks lying in a hospital bed watching the homework she was too weak to do piling up and relying on everyone's pity to carry her through.

Or maybe not ever doing the homework, she thought on those mornings she woke up before Dad, lying in the dark feeling lonely and freezing cold inside. Maybe lying down in the hospital bed and knowing she'd never get up again, knowing that her small, frail body could only take so much.

She didn't want to die, she wasn't ready, she had too much to do. Sometimes she thought about what Eccles said, and she did feel good for a while. Maybe just being alive was its own justification. Maybe the love she felt for Dad and for all her friends made her life worthwhile.

But the comfort she got from this idea never lasted very long.

Still, she was grateful to Eccles. Lots of people had helped her and supported her, but Eccles was the only one who had told her stuff that made her feel better, that helped her to see things in a different way, that changed the way she thought about things.

She knew she couldn't do any of that stuff for him, but maybe there was one thing she could do.

Later that week, she was sitting at Melville's with Adam, Melissa, and Stephanie. She and Stephanie had just finished quizzing each other on the finer points of the Slab of Tedium, and she turned to Adam, who was typing yet another AP English paper on his laptop, and said, "Hey, can you look somebody up for me?"

"Yeah, sure," Adam said. "I need a break from Hester Prynne anyway."

Brianna looked at him blankly. "Sorry," he said. "Who is it?"

"Grace Eccles. In California," she said.

"Is that . . ."

"It's his daughter." She watched as Adam tap-tap-tapped the name into his computer.

"Okay. There is no Grace Eccles listed in California. Let me just try G." Brianna started to feel embarrassed. This whole thing was dumb. If Grace was married, she would probably have a different last name, and she might even have ditched the last name of the dad she hated in any case. But then Adam responded, "There are two G. Eccleses in California. One in Palo Alto and one in Glendale."

"I guess you'd better give me both of them." Adam read off the addresses, and Brianna copied them down.

"What are you doing, Bri?" Stephanie asked.

Brianna initially didn't know how to answer without getting into infinitesimals, the beauty of mathematics, and the mysteries of prime numbers.

"Mr. Eccles told me that his daughter doesn't speak to him, and I just feel kind of bad for him, so I thought I would write her a letter." Adam, Melissa, and Stephanie all stared at her without saying anything. "Yeah, I guess it's a little weird."

"A little?" Melissa said.

"Do you have a crush on the fat guy?" Stephanie asked.

"No, I do not have a— You know, it is possible to care about somebody without having a crush on them."

Adam raised an eyebrow like this was a point of view that had never occurred to him.

That night after dinner, Brianna finished her homework and then got out a sheet of notebook paper.

Dear Grace Eccles, she wrote,

First, I'm sorry if you aren't Grace Eccles, or if you are Grace Eccles but not the one whose dad is John Eccles, a math teacher in Blackpool, Massachusetts.

I wanted to let you know that your dad is dying, or, anyway, has serious heart trouble. He is still working and everything, but his heart is pretty well shot, so it's only a matter of time.

I am one of his students. He's helped me a lot with two things. One of them is math, which I guess isn't that big of a deal, except that I really don't think I've ever had a teacher as good as him in thirteen years of school. The other thing he's helped me with is thinking about life. And death. Which probably sounds like I'm a dippy teenage girl to you, but I have cystic fibrosis, so I've had some friends die, and I know my odds of living to your age are pretty slim.

He told me some of the story of how he split up with your mom. If he was my dad, I'd still be mad at him, too. But I just wanted you to know that even

though he was a horrible dad for you, I think maybe
he changed my life.

I have a mom who let me down, who left because
she couldn't deal with me being sick. I hate her for
that. My dad says I don't owe her anything, and I
guess you don't owe your dad anything either, but I
do just want you to know that if you wanted to tell
him something nice, even if you didn't really mean it,
he might die a little bit less sad.

I'm sorry for butting into your personal business,
but, like I said, your dad helped me a lot, and I just
wanted to try to do something nice for him and this
was all I could think of. I'm sorry if I upset you. I
won't bug you about this again.

Thanks.

Sincerely,

Brianna Pelletier

Once she was done, she wrote it all out again, and she mailed a
letter to each of the G. Eccleses in California. Now she was thinking about whether she ought to write to Mom.

She went and found Dad on the couch watching some show
about a female detective he had a crush on.

"I don't know why you like this show. She's kind of funny-
looking."

"I enjoy the mystery aspect, okay?" Dad said. "Did you come
out here just to make fun of Kyra Sedgwick?"

Brianna smiled. "No, I was wondering if I should write to
Mom or something."

Dad turned off the TV. "Well, she would certainly appreciate it. How would *you* feel about it?"

"I don't know. I was thinking that there might be some good stuff about her even though she's a horrible mom."

Dad thought about that for a second. "Yeah, there's some good stuff about her. She was actually a lot of fun."

"Eww, Dad, I don't want to hear about my conception."

Dad blushed. "That's not what I meant. You know how there are some people that are just fun to be around? Maybe they're not very good friends, and they're not reliable, but you always want them there when you go out, because they make it more fun?"

Brianna knew a few of those people, but she'd stopped hanging out with them. She told him yes.

"Well, your mom's like that."

Brianna chewed on that. "I don't know what to say to her because I feel like I should write and say I forgive her, but I'm not sure I do."

"Maybe you don't have to forgive her. I mean, I know this makes me a bad person, but I don't think she's earned your forgiveness. But maybe you could just tell her about going to MIT—"

"Dad, I haven't gotten in. You need to stop saying that."

"Okay. But seriously, I think anything from you would mean a lot to her, and you don't have to get into anything deep. Just say hi."

Brianna thought it would be weird to be so casual, but then again, if she waited until she forgave Mom for leaving, she'd never ever write to her. And Brianna was starting to feel like hating Mom was taking more energy than she had.

"Well, maybe I will. But not tonight. I've gotta go to sleep. I'll let you get back to your girlfriend."

Dad got up and hugged her. "Good night, sweetie. You're my favorite person on earth."

Brianna hugged him back and went to bed.

such a good life

Brianna didn't write to Mom that day or the next, or for several weeks after that. A new year began, and January came and went. One day she was talking to Ashley after school when her phone rang. She looked and saw that it was Adam. "Fat envelope!" he said.

"Oh my God! Congratulations!"

"Thanks! Is yours there?"

"I'm not home," Brianna replied, and she said goodbye and ran to the Sunfire. When she got home, she too had a fat envelope from MIT, complete with a generous financial aid package.

Dad was so proud she thought he might literally explode. "This is your lucky day, Bri! Your bike's done, too."

Brianna's heart leapt, and she ran to the garage. She knew Dad was short on both time and money and was spending a lot of both on her bike, so she had decided not to hassle him about when it would be done. But there it was, in the middle of the garage with its chrome pipes shining and gas-tank orca looking cool and menacing. Just for a minute, it seemed like it was telling her to ride into the future.

Dad insisted on taking her out to dinner to celebrate. They rode Brianna's new motorcycle, and Dad let her take a few spins around the parking lot. Of course, he wouldn't let her ride it on the street until she had a license and insurance, and even then he probably wouldn't let her on the bike if there was so much as a drop of rain on the pavement.

Eccles was happy for her. He had dropped some weight and looked better than he had at his worst, but he still didn't really look good. "Ms. Pelletier," he said, "I should congratulate the institution on the wisdom of their decision, but congratulations to you, too."

Now that she'd gotten into MIT, she felt like she could write to Mom.

Dear Mom,

Hi. I just wanted to write you and let you know that I got into MIT, so, if all goes well, that's where I'll be in the fall. Otherwise, school is fine, although now that I'm into college it's going to be hard to stay motivated. I hope you're well. I'm not so great right now—I'm due for a tune-up. Hopefully I'll be all set for the fall, though.

Take care,
Brianna

She didn't sign off with "love," because she felt like that was exaggerating, and you couldn't really sign off a letter with "absence of hate." She mailed the letter, and after she'd dropped it into the mailbox, it felt like she'd just let go of something as heavy as she was. Weird.

Weeks went by, and it got harder and harder to breathe. Brianna wondered if anybody who didn't have CF ever stopped to think about how great it was that they could breathe without working at it, without thinking about it. Probably not. It wasn't like she spent a lot of time thinking about how great it was that she could walk, except when she saw Keith Who Is in a Wheelchair.

She toughed it out as much as she could, brushed off everybody's questions about how she was feeling, until one night she was lying on the couch and she started to feel feverish.

She wanted to get up, do some homework, maybe have a snack, do something that would show she was okay. She must have fallen asleep because she woke up with Dad in her face, pressing his forehead against hers. "Jesus, you're burning up," he said, reaching for the phone.

"Dad, I'm fine, I was just tired. Don't call, I don't wanna go in. I don't want to."

Dad paused while dialing. "I know, sweetie. I'm sorry. I wish to God you didn't have to."

"Dammit," Brianna said, and fell back asleep.

Then Dad was lifting her into the car. "I'm not ready," she said. "I want to go to college." And, she thought, I want to ride my orca bike to my dorm.

"Shh . . ." Dad said. "You will, Bri. But tonight we're going to the hospital."

She slept again, and then just caught bits and pieces of whatever was happening: the sound of the wipers as the rain fell; a prick as an IV went into her arm; waking up afraid with the oxygen mask over her face and saying "Daddy?" and Dad waking up and assuring her, "It's okay, pumpkin, go back to sleep," and brushing her hair with his hand.

At some point, she heard Dr. Patel talking to Dad. Something about how she really wasn't in good enough shape for a transplant, and if they'd put her on the list last year when she suggested . . . She faded out.

She woke up and it was dark, but gray light was just starting to peek under the window shades. She saw Dad's silhouette in the chair next to her bed.

She knew that her fever had broken, and she was happy to be clearheaded because she knew just as surely that she was never going to leave this room.

She'd lain awake so many early mornings, being afraid that she might die, and now that she knew it—really knew it in her bones—she was surprised to find that she wasn't afraid. She used to worry that she would die before graduation, that she would die before her senior prom, and then that she'd die before she got to attend any classes at MIT. And now that it was certain that she'd die without a diploma, without a hideous prom dress in her closet, without ever getting the ugly MIT ring with the beaver on it, none of that stuff seemed important at all. She'd gotten less time than most people, but it had been pretty good time, and looking back at it now, she didn't feel any regret. She had good friends, she'd had a lot of fun, and having kids, growing up, all that stuff was like sky-diving—she was going to die without ever getting to do it, but that fact didn't particularly bother her.

She didn't know what was coming next, but, finally, the thing Dad had always said was really comforting: "Whatever happens, you won't be sick anymore." She was tired of treatments, she was tired of medication, of percussion, and the hospital. If she had a choice, she wouldn't go, but there was definitely a part of her that was relieved.

"Dad," she said.

Dad woke up instantly and reached for her hand. "Hey, pumpkin. It's good to see you."

"You, too." She sat there for just a second feeling Dad's hand around hers and feeling really lucky that he'd been her dad. "Dad, you have to call people."

Dad smiled. "Bri, your phone has been ringing off the hook for two days. Everyone knows."

Two days? Wow. She really would have thought it was the morning after she'd come to the hospital. But two days would explain the stubble all over Dad's face. "Oh. But, I mean, tell them I need to see them. I need to say goodbye."

Dad's face looked pained. "Sweetie, stop that. Dr. Patel said with enough treatment now, they can probably get you in shape for a lung transplant. I mean I got you on the list and—"

"Dad, I don't want a transplant. It's done. I'm done. I can't do this anymore."

"I . . ." Dad said, but then he was crying and he couldn't talk, and Brianna felt bad.

"I'm sorry," she said. "I'm sorry I've been such a burden to you. I'm sorry you didn't get the life you wanted."

Dad looked up. "Bri, shut up," he said through his tears. "You're the best thing that ever happened to me. You made me a much better person, and every single day . . . every day you've been in my life you've made me happier than I ever thought I would get to be."

Brianna smiled and squeezed Dad's hand. Finally Dad sniffed and said, "Okay. So, who do you want me to call?"

"Melissa. Stephanie. Adam. And Eccles. Mr. Eccles, my math teacher. I don't have his number, but his first name is John. He lives in Blackpool."

Dad looked surprised. "Anyone else?"

Brianna thought about it. "Nah," she replied. "I don't think so. Ashley, but she won't be allowed to come anyway. In fact, will you . . . will you just keep everybody else away?"

"Sure," he said. "I'll do that."

"Why don't you go get some breakfast and call them? I think I need to rest some more."

Dad looked uncertain. "Okay, pumpkin. I love you."

"I love you too, Daddy."

Brianna went back to sleep.

She woke up and saw Adam sitting in a chair next to Dad. She wondered for a minute how he'd gotten here before anybody else when he didn't have a car. She thought dimly that she was probably on morphine, and she felt weird and muddleheaded.

"Hey," she said.

"Hey," Adam answered softly.

"Um, Dad, can you give us a minute?" Dad looked like he really didn't want to go. "Dad, I promise I won't croak while you're out of the room."

"Jeez, Bri," he said. Then he said, "Adam, you want something horrible to eat or drink from the cafeteria? Some coffee?"

"Sure," Adam said, "some coffee would be good. Black, please." He was digging in his pockets for money, but Dad waved his hand and left.

"So," Adam said when Dad had gone.

"So," Brianna said, and there was so much she wanted to say, but talking required breathing, and that was just too hard right now. "Thanks," she managed.

"Yeah, well," Adam said, "you're my best friend, you know, and I love you."

Brianna smiled. She thought about how, even if he'd said that last week, she would have wondered if he meant *love* love, or just like friend love, and what that meant, and whether things were going to change between them, and whether she was attracted to him or anything. But now, none of that seemed important at all. "You too," she responded, because she did. Adam smiled.

There was so much more she wanted to say: When you graduate and get rich, maybe you can name something at MIT after me, don't feel bad if you hook up with Stephanie or Melissa . . . Too much talking, too much effort.

Adam filled the silence. "I . . . You've made this year so much fun for me, so much better than any other year of my whole life. I'm so glad I got to know you."

Brianna just nodded and pointed at him.

"Um . . ." Adam looked like he had something else he wanted to say. Brianna wondered what it could possibly be—he'd already told her he loved her. "Is it . . . Would it . . . Can I kiss you?"

"Yes," Brianna answered.

Adam reached over and slowly, tenderly, lifted up her oxygen mask and gave her a soft, sweet kiss. Then he leaned back and put the mask back on.

"Thanks. That was nice," she said, smiling and drifting away.

When she woke up again, Melissa and Stephanie were sitting there. "Hi," she said.

"Hey," Melissa said quietly.

"Ready to go home yet?" Stephanie said.

Brianna just looked at her. "No." That was all it took to start both of her friends crying.

Melissa finally said, "Bri, is there anything you want? Is there anything you want us to do for you?"

"Don't leave. I love you."

Suddenly they were both hugging her from either side of the bed. "We love you, too."

Melissa and Stephanie sat back down. They were all silent for a while.

"Talk about something," Brianna said.

Melissa and Stephanie wiped their faces and took turns telling her about how Emma and Charles broke up, and then about how Emma had called Denise a backstabbing slut when she started making out with Charles, and at some point, Brianna fell asleep, feeling happy.

She had a hazy vision of Eccles standing there with Dad, but she was too weak to wake up all the way, and then she was asleep again.

When she woke up, Dad was back in the room with Melissa and Stephanie and Adam. Melissa went down to the cafeteria to get them some dinner, and everybody but Brianna ate. She wasn't hungry. She wondered kind of abstractly if she'd ever eat again. She found she didn't much care one way or the other.

Dad held her hand, and Brianna closed her eyes. Now that she'd said all her goodbyes, she was ready to go, and as she drifted off to sleep, she felt happy that she'd had such a good life.

She was surprised when she woke up the next morning. Well, she reflected, her body had never really done exactly what she thought it should, so there was probably no reason for it to start now.

She lay in bed the whole day, and Adam and Stephanie and Melissa came back, and it was nice just to be with all of her favorite people, and Brianna wanted so much to tell them how much she loved them, how much she appreciated them, what a gift this extra day was, how there was no way she'd rather spend her last day alive than with them. But it was too much, and every time she tried to say it, she just started to cough. Finally Dad leaned over really close and said, "You don't have to say it, pumpkin. We know. And we all love you, too."

Day turned into night, and Adam and Stephanie and Melissa left, and only Dad remained, holding her hand and singing her songs he used to sing to her when she was a little kid. It was perfect.

sudden silence

Inside the room, Stephen Pelletier knew Brianna had died by the sudden silence where her labored breathing had been.

In the hallway outside the room, the nurses knew Brianna Pelletier had died by the great gulping sobs coming from the big man holding the small, lifeless body of his precious daughter.

beautifully

John Eccles, wearing a suit from his closet so old it now qualified as vintage, walked up the steps to the pulpit. Every seat was full, and most people were crying. In the middle, Ashley sat between her mother and father. In the front row, Brianna's father and her three best friends sat together, holding hands. In the very last pew, Brianna's mother sat alone.

John Eccles reached into his suit jacket, pulled out what he'd written, and smoothed it onto the podium. The microphone picked up the sound of crinkling paper and broadcast it to the congregation. He took a deep breath, and then he began to speak.

"I was Brianna's calculus teacher. One thing we learn in calculus class is the value of infinitesimals. I won't bore you with the details, but, essentially, quantities which are very small are incredibly important.

"So it is with Brianna's life. Though she lived a short time—an incredibly short time, to my old brain's way of thinking—let us not measure the value of Brianna's life by its length. Let us not say, if only she had done this, if only she had done that, if only she'd lived to do x, y, or z. The fact that you are sitting here today means that you were touched by Brianna Pelletier, that her life was valuable to you no matter its length. Perhaps she touched you with her kindness; perhaps she inspired you with her intelligence; perhaps she brightened your day with her sense of humor; perhaps, in her generosity, she gave you her own bottle of an electric-blue sports drink.

"Whatever the case, you know that Brianna's life was precious, valuable, wonderful. So let us not think about what Brianna didn't do. Let us think, instead, of what she did, of the ways in which she touched us all. Let us hope that, someday, we too may touch people as she has done.

"When we lose someone important to us, we feel their absence as a horrible void inside of us, a void that will never be filled. They are dancing in infinity, but we long for their presence, and we struggle to understand the best way to honor our memory of them.

"What would Brianna have us do? How can we live so as to honor her, to honor the role she played in our lives, her importance to us? Those of you who are still alive in five, ten, fifteen, fifty, sixty years, living lives so far removed from Brianna, how will you honor her as she deserves to be honored?

"I propose we honor Brianna's unfairly brief life and her importance to us by striving to live as she lived: by being courageous and doing things that are difficult for us, things we are afraid of. By living vibrantly, as she did, by celebrating our talents and planning for a future that is uncertain for all of us, by not letting those things which are hard for us deter us from experiencing all we want to experience. And first, and foremost, by being kind and loving to one another, so that when we, too, come to die, we shall be missed as sorely and painfully as we now miss Brianna. We can honor her by living our lives as she did hers: beautifully."

John Eccles stepped down from the podium. The pastor asked everyone to rise and join in "How Can I Keep From Singing." As the congregation sang, Stephen Pelletier, shoulders heaving with grief, bore the urn containing his daughter's ashes from the church. Behind him, crying and still clutching each other's hands as though to keep from sinking into a sea of despair, walked Stephanie St. Pierre, Adam Pennington, and Melissa D'Amico.

Three thousand miles from Blackpool, a woman picked up her phone and called her father. He didn't answer, and she left a message.

Day turned into night, and, at two o'clock in the morning, Melissa, Stephanie, and Adam walked to the moonlit beach. Each carried a small container of ashes given to them by Stephen Pelletier. Drunk on grief and tequila, each of them dipped a hand into their own container of ashes, drew out a handful, and sprinkled it onto the sea.

"Goodbye," Adam Pennington said through his tears. They stood and watched in the moonlight as the waves lapped unceasingly at the shore and the tiny cloud of ashes that had once been part of the body of Brianna Pelletier dispersed, each particle now floating amid a number of water molecules as close to infinite as the human mind could comprehend.

∞

Twenty-five miles away, a graduate student sat in a basement at the Massachusetts Institute of Technology, grateful to have been able to book any time at all on the supercomputer, even the hours between two and four a.m. on Sunday morning. As the ashes that had once been the body of Brianna Pelletier struck the water in Blackpool, a supercomputer in a basement in Cambridge running a program written by a graduate student sent a signal to a monitor.

The monitor displayed a number.

The number was incredibly large.

The number was prime, and no human being had ever seen it before.

acknowledgments

Thanks to Suzanne Demarco for helping me to live and write more beautifully.

Thanks to Dana Reinhardt, who helped me find this book inside a sprawling mess of a first draft.

Thanks to Janine O'Malley for believing in this book and for working so hard to help me make it better.

Thanks to Doug Stewart for ongoing friendship, encouragement, and general awesomeness.

Thanks to Trish Cook for thoughtful and helpful feedback.

Thanks to Casey Nelson, Rowen Halpin, and Kylie Nelson for inspiration.

Thanks to Arthur Lee and all the members of Love for the title and for music that moved me, Adam, and Brianna.